BEN'S
WAYNE

Levi Miller

Good Books

Intercourse, Pennsylvania 17534

Design and cover by Cheryl Benner.

Ben's Wayne

© 1989 by Good Books, Intercourse, PA 17534
International Standard Book Number: 0-934672-77-6
Library of Congress Catalog Card Number: 89-32436

Library of Congress Cataloging-in-Publication Data
Miller, Levi.
    Ben's Wayne/Levi Miller.
        p.   cm.
    ISBN 0-934672-77-6: $14.95
    I. Title.
PS3563.I4137B46   1989   89-32436
813'.54 — dc20   CIP

Blessed are the meek, for they shall inherit the earth.
—*Jesus, Matthew 5:5*
Rent a farm, milk cows, learn a trade if possible, do manual labor as did Paul, and all that which you then fall short of will doubtlessly be given and provided you by pious brethren.
—*Menno Simons, 1496–1561*
The Westerners are civilized barbarians, so they have nothing more to live for. It would be as aberrant for us to imitate them as for a stalwart, hard-working healthy young man to envy a rich Parisian who is bald at thirty and sits in his townhouse moaning, "Ah, how tedious it all is!" He is to be pitied, not envied.
—*Leo Tolstoy, 1828–1910*
Among material resources, the greatest, unquestionably, is the land. Study how a society uses its land, and you can come to pretty reliable conclusions as to what its future will be.
—*E.F. Schumacher, 1911–1977*

This story is true, but it is not factual. Although everything in this fictitious story could have happened, none of it describes any specific person or family in a factual manner.

The four stanzas of the Michael Sattler hymn in Chapter 7 are excerpted directly from the *Ausbund* (available from Pathway Publishers, Aylmer, Ontario) as noted in the text and from *The Legacy of Michael Sattler* by John H. Yoder (Herald Press, 1973), pages 140–143. The English translation is the author's attempt at versification of the German text.

1.

I was going home from Anna's on the graveyard road north of Holmesburg. My black mare with a white star on the forehead trotted along at an even gait. Like a sleepy old cluck, I sat in the buggy and listened to the music of the wheels. Two wheels in the loose gravel sent the stones crackling apart in scratching tones. The other two rubber wheels on the blacktop moved quietly with the singing sound of a woman's lullaby.

My eyes opened a wink to see the bright battery headlights shine in the early morning darkness, but then the scratching and singing tones made me *duddlich* and my eyes closed again. *Duddlich?* I don't know how to say it in English right, but it's when the lower jaw drops down, you get all relaxed and, who knows, you might even drip a little water from the mouth, kind of like a contented dog.

My large black mare was Flecha. Even in my buggy sleep I could feel her steadily move up the hill. Her nostrils were bright pink-red on the inside and wide open, blowing out big puffs of warm air. She looked like a four-legged locomotive with the white steam clouds around her face. For a year now we had taken this route home every Sunday morning, and she knew exactly where we were going.

I didn't actually see her because I was sleeping the way you can in a buggy, even if you shouldn't sleep like that. But Judas, it was hard to stay awake. Anyway, Flecha really didn't need directions because she was smart, loyal and fast.

Ja, I liked my horse and even bragged a little that she had run a two o four at the Northfield Track. That's a pretty nice clip. And that was when she was a two- and three-year-old. Now, at six and after two colts, her speed had slowed down some, but her smarts had not gone down. Her loyalty and strength were better than ever, plus she had a three-month-old foal at home that she wanted to see.

But I wasn't mainly dreaming of Flecha that morning. My dreaming sleep would show pictures, and then I would open my eyes and there was my horse. In my sleep I saw a young woman asleep, a soaring hawk and some ducks caught in the buggy spokes. These pictures blurred and the scenes changed, and then there were more ducks and feathers. By gum, those feathers got in my eyes and were floating all over the place. It was like a broiler house filled with feathers but no chickens.

Then the picture of the young woman came up clearer to me. She was asleep in bed, and her eyes were closed. But underneath they were moving. They were black and alive. The mouth was open just a little, and if I looked closely at her lips, they moved just a little. Her arms hung loosely beside her lean body, but her fingers were moving. Her legs were slim and firm and reached toward her feet and toes which were long but not skinny.

Ja, if I tried I could see them. The toes were also twitching. Ah, Anna, even in your sleep you are wide awake. You could never hold still.

But my close looking of all those details didn't hold, and then I just saw her lying on her stomach, her handsome face to the side.

She's a Holstein, Chris used to say. *Ja*, that's true and shouldn't a farmer be attached to a Holstein rather than some little Jersey? But she was a fence jumper too. I knew it the first time I saw her at a wedding Roy and I went to over near Breman. The young women were not supposed to be looking over at the *Buwe*. But she did. Her dark eyes would jump about like little calves in the springtime.

A small part of my white hanky hung out of my pants pocket when I walked past the group of girls. She said, "Does he want to get out?"

Just like that, she said it. "Uh," I only grunted. I never was good at answering just like that off the top of my head. But then, I said, "*Ja*, he wants to see too." But then I got red in the face and stuffed the hanky deep down in my pocket.

How that little comment enchanted me. It charged me up for the rest of the evening, even if they put me to eating the midnight dinner with that dainty little Sarah. Little Jersey that she was, with dimples you could have put strawberries into the holes.

"Does he want to get out? " What a thing to say about my hanky. It was a special one, of course. It had my initials W.W. on the corners and was a Christmas gift from my father. They were stiched in old script that looked a little like the fraktur my father Ben could write. My father — he's another story — and I had to get away from him before I could appreciate him.

Anyway, Dad's name was Benjamin, but everyone just called him Ben. He gave me the hanky for Christmas. He always gave us hankies for Christmas — to everyone: sons, in-laws, grandsons, everyone. We said he was either too tight to give anything else or he didn't know any better. Anyway, I was glad to have the hanky that evening.

I should have told Anna that my hanky wants to get out to meet her little hanky. She had a little white embroidered one tucked under her breasts sticking out from her cape. But I didn't think of it fast enough, and it doesn't matter a hoot now after two years. Still I often thought of our meeting of the hankies — hers under the cape and mine sticking out from the pants pocket.

Then that first meeting went away, and there were clouds and then I saw her face by itself. It was calm, but when I looked closely at the lips which I could only see from the side, they were twitching slightly and smiling.

Anna went away again and more clouds came billowing by and then a hawk showed up. Red-tailed — or broad shouldered, I couldn't see it that well — soared with the air currents and moved up and down slightly. Then he was gone.

I clicked my tongue, tslch, tslch. Even with my eyes closed, I saw my black horse hold a steady line down the right side of the road. I saw the curved lean neck and the little head held forward, alert and light.

Ah, my good horse, hold to the road and keep a steady gait. You are both alive and alert and also stay on the road. You are the animal Anna. I couldn't say anything nicer about you, either of you. Tslch, tslch, my tongue went. You are so alive and I'm so sleepy.

Then the clouds came back, billowing and bringing feathers, I saw white feathers and black and grey feathers. Then along came bills and wings and eyes and tails, and I spotted the shapes of Muscovy ducks, Chris Yoder's ducks.

I had killed one that morning at Chris's place. Dirty things were sitting out by the drive like usual. They always sat around there and made a commotion, but that morning they got excited and came hissing and half flying across the drive, and we ran over a few.

I wanted to keep right on going and let them die in peace, but it would not have been right with Chris and Martha. What with his being my brother-in-law and all. So I stopped Flecha and made the rest of the *Buwe* stop too, and we went back to the door with the dead duck.

Chris was mad, I could tell even if he didn't want to let it on. Not that I blame him that much. Who wants to be awoken at five o'clock in the morning on the off-Sunday. My sister Martha stood behind him like a white outline in the darkness.

"Sure *Buwe*, we'll take care of that. You just have a safe ride home now." That's what he said and I left. But I knew what would happen next. I even heard him growl when we turned around to leave. "That's what we get with this all-night courtship and running around."

I didn't hear any more, but I knew he would carry on about poor education, bad morals, radiant heat, bed courtship and the future of the four little ones, their sons. And if that weren't enough, what with the whole District being legalistic and going nowhere. Those ducks were the projects of his sons. Why aren't they out here needing to clean up the mess when they have all these projects from ducks to banties to hoopies and never take care of them. I knew Martha would listen to all that, most of which was true, and then still say, "Now, let's go clean the duck."

"Howeeeeeee!" The milkman Toots Hacker passed me and must have seen me sleeping. He tooted the horn and shouted like some hyena right out of Africa. Flecha gave a quick jump sideways but did not bolt. I opened my eyes in time to see the truck flash past, hauling "nature's most perfect food," as the big letters on the back claimed. The truck backfired as it slowed down for the stop sign ahead.

Dumma Ding, why can't you let a man sleep and rest on a Sunday morning. There ought to be a law about people like you. Don't some places have rules about noise? But what do you expect from Toots?

My eyelids dropped again and by the time we reached the top of the hill and the reddish sun brightened the morning, I was back to sleepytown. Again the hawk showed up in the air currents, ducks squawked and everything changed to a swirling blue color.

Do you always have to sit right in the middle of the drive? Squawk you oily hissers. You corkscrews. You ugly ducklings. Chris doesn't like you anyway. Swimming on a pond, that's where you belong. Chris's boys need a pond for you. Then you wouldn't get into our buggy spokes and lose your heads. Black and grey blurs came in my head again, and all kinds of shapes were flying around.

Tslch, tslch, my tongue clicked to my horse, even as I slept and woke. The sun was now a small bright red ball on top of the eastern hills around the valley of Holmesburg. Its warmth came in the side of the buggy and warmed my cheeks.

Two miles further down the road Flecha took a right turn and headed in the lane. The buggy bounced and jumped up and down on the rough drive, but I stayed *duddlich*. Flecha pricked up her ears and gave two short whinnies, kind of like a locomotive tooting our arrival; we were pulling up to the station. Bounce came running across the open pasture field, barking like all get out.

Bounce's happy barking finally woke me up, and I opened my eyes and saw the ugly short-haired terrier plus McCollough's mutt come racing at us. I took the reins, guiding Flecha slightly to the left to miss a bump.

"Whoa, Flecha, easy, easy," I talked to her, trying to make up for the past half hour of sleeping when she'd been trotting along without my help.

Tslch, tslch. I clicked my tongue and leaned back again. The sun was bright and my body felt warm as toast.

Ah, what a life this is. I'll have a dog too, fields of wheat and corn like this . . . cows, *ja*, all Guernsies purebred and maybe even a few sheep. No, they won't make money, but they'll add to the farm. Anyway, we'll have a meadow and they can keep it trimmed. And I'll need some work horses — or, of course, we could buy some mules, a little cheaper wouldn't founder and all that.

What did I do to deserve all this? I have a beautiful woman, a faithful horse, godly parents, and this good-for-nothing dog running across the pasture barking his head off. *Lieber Gott*, how blessed I am.

Those were my good thoughts. Too good, I knew when I saw the back end of a '55 Chevy sticking out from behind the shed. No, it was not all so good. There was my brother's car, and he was wild and had joined the army. He wanted to get out and stay out. And Anna, did she want to get out? Sometimes, deep underneath, I thought my woman did. All the *Buwe* acted as if they were ready to get cars and take off. And even I wanted to go sometimes. If this was such a good place why did everyone want to leave?

Benny came running out from the barn and almost ran right in front of Flecha. And why did one of my brothers have to be born without any brains? "Whoa, whoa," he called.

Flecha moved to the front of the barn and parked us under the overhang. As I unhitched her, she whinnied now and then to her foal which she smelled inside in the stalls. I led Flecha into the barn and her iron shoes clip-clopped loud echoes on the cement. Leona came out from behind a cow, and I could see the rest of my family spread out under the udders doing the morning milking.

"You're still in time to help with the last four cows," said Leona. I nodded and headed for the milkhouse.

2.

The milking had warmed me, and I felt fresh and alive as I walked to the house. The sun felt warm on my back. *Ja*, today would be a good day to go fishing. I promised the Yoder boys I would take them fishing today so we wanted some warmth and a breeze. A few clouds might help, but mainly we wanted sun and fresh air.

Bounce greeted me on the bare dirt patch along the side of the front porch. He kept this spot hard and clean by whacking the ground with his little tail like the flapping of a rubber band motor.

Ah, my wild dog, *wie gehts* this morning? Where were you last night? Off to some party or did you have some bitch by yourself on the back forty? Or were you up in Wooster seeing some of those English girls? I reached down to pat the terrior-hound and he licked my hand, the water dripping from the hinges of his mouth.

Inside I smelled the fresh coffee. *Die Memm* was at the stove heating some chicken for the noon dinner and Ben was at the kitchen sink splashing his face with the cold water. Standing behind my father, I could see his thin hair come over the back of his collar. But when he bent down over the bowl, I could see his white neck. Ben shook his head and snorted like a pig in a trough.

"He's still not up." He said it with water sloshing through his mouth.

"Came in late," I said.

"*Ja*, way late, clammered around the door and woke us all." Some more splashes of water. "And then he went down to the cellar. He was drunk. *Ja*, went down to the basement and was looking for the dandelion wine. *Litterlich*, I say, *litterlich*."

My father continued: "Can you imagine, after he was out drinking all night, he comes home and wants to drink our dandelion wine." My father was now drying his face, but he was still blowing and snorting.

"*Ja*, I don't know why he does these things," I said. "Seems he's not in control of himself."

"*Vell*, I told him to get out of there and stop stealing."

"You can't be a thief in your own house, can you?" I said.

"*Ja vell*, this isn't his house anymore. He has left us and he's just like an outsider. You can only have one home, and he has another one now."

"Are you sure he has another home?" I tried to cool him down, but it didn't do any good.

"You bet he does, or if not, he can find one pretty fast. Judas River, anyway he's *litterlich* — getting into the Army and then coming home here and not working and now getting drunk and stealing our wine." Ben sat down and pulled up his chair in a loud, hard, scraping noise. "And after all the money we have given him."

"Mary, is the coffee hot? Bring it over here. Leona, where are you? Benny, come over here beside me. John, sit down. Sit down." He looked closer at Benny, his youngest son who carried his name. "Now you aren't washed. Now get over to the spigot and get that manure off your hands."

We sat down to the breakfast and the sunlight came in the window, but now it all seemed dark to me. I, who had felt good about the morning, now felt terrible. My father jerked his hand to his chin the way he always did when he was nervous or mad. How he hated Roy. It was like a cloud of bad gas. I kept my mouth shut during the rest of the breakfast, and then I went up to my room.

It was a mess. Clothes were all over the floor and shoes and socks spread around the room. This was always the way the room looked when Roy came home. He threw everything around. Roy was lying on his back in the middle of the bed with only a pair of shorts on. His long ducktail hair hung down over the one ear like a fender skirt.

"What's the old man growling about?"

"Says you were after his wine last night."

"What does it matter? A little wine is good for you. Why else do we have it there?"

"*Vell,* he didn't put it there for you." Now I was on my father's side. "Anyway, you should have asked him for it."

"Asking that stubborn mule for something is like asking a stone for water. You know how tight he is. You'll never see anything coming out of him. Why, he's so tight he'd plant corn on the lane to get more money. You'd better believe it."

I started to pick up his socks and hung his pants on a hook. "*Ja vell,* that's why we have money and a farm," I said. "You have to save sometimes."

"Who cares about a farm when you don't enjoy it? What is money but a way of getting enjoyment? That's what these people have never learned, how to enjoy themselves. But that's what you need. What is life, but a chance to be happy."

"*Ja vell,* we do enjoy it here. We enjoy animals, the land, and a quiet and peaceful life. That's why we save and have some money."

"Shoot, the wine was there to drink so why not drink it? Who will ever miss it? I haven't had dandelion for a long time." That was his last point, and he jumped out of bed.

His voice changed to a friendly tone when he asked me: "What are you up to today?"

"I'll go fishing with the Yoders. Some of the *Buwe* are going swimming."

"Maybe I'll drop over by later in the afternoon," he said, and I thought of how nice my brother could be.

My younger brother John and I walked over to the Yoders, and we all went fishing over at Mony Hershberger's pond. John was actually just two years younger than I was, but I was closer to Leona and in some ways to the little nephews than to John. I think John kept a little distance just to make sure we weren't the same. Roy was 22, I was 18, Leona 17 and John 16 and Benny was 11.

I also had three older married sisters: Martha 32, May 29 and Esther 25. Martha married Chris and they had three little ones who were about 10 to 12 and little Samuel who wasn't in school yet. I could never keep their ages straight.

Anyway, our young nephews were as excited as spring pullets about the fishing. We walked the several miles to Hershbergers, and they were talking a blue streak about the big bass that got away from Aden last week and about the duck that the *Buwe* had killed in the drive. Aden got a spinning rod for his twelfth birthday and had caught one big largemouth with it, about 15 inches. Then last week he had reeled in another even bigger one, but just as he had the net out to scoop it in, it got away. John winked at me as they went over it for the fifteenth time, but I just listened. I was always a sucker for people to tell me things like that.

Anyway, I was more interested in what they had to say about those *Buwe* who had killed one of their projects. I didn't tell them I had hit one of them, and they sounded just like their father in how bad the *Buwe* were in staying out till way late, then killing one of their ducks and wounding a few more.

Aden and I cast with the spinning rods while Raymond and Matthew fished with worms and poles for bluegills, and John soon headed for the swimming hole at the other end of the pond. Matthew all at once looked over to me and said, "Wayne, do you think Daniel will ever come home again?"

"I hope so."

"I'd like to go up there again."

"Why didn't you go with your mom and dad?" I asked.

"They didn't want us along. Said we could go later again. I had never seen anything like that."

"What the whips and the chicken fence?" asked Raymond.

"That and a man like Daniel." Matthew moved his pole to another part of the water. "What makes a man go crazy?"

"They say he was always a little strange," I said.

"*Ja,* but not like that," said Matthew. "He used to be good friends with Dad and they say he was just regular then." He lifted his pole and hook all the way out of the water and turned to me.

"Do you think it could happen to Dad? It's his family. Maybe Dad will get it, and then one of us will go crazy too. We already have one who isn't quite all there."

Aden started talking pretty serious now. "No, you don't get it from family breeding. You get it from the way you live."

"I know but his side of the family has a lot more of those things," said Matthew. "Remember when Ezra hung himself, and everybody knows that Elizabeth is crazy."

"You don't know what you're talking about." Aden talked some more, "Daniel's only related by marriage so he isn't really related. And Elizabeth isn't crazy; she's just nervous, like an Ayrshire."

"But I feel it sometimes," continued Matthew. "I could go crazy."

"Only if you just think about it all the time. That's what *die Memm* says."

"But how do I keep from it?"

"Just don't do it."

"But your mind isn't like that. It doesn't always do what you want it to do."

"Yes, you can," continued Aden. "Usually you can if you try. Think about fishing."

Raymond helped out then by changing the subject. "I've got a nibble again," he said as his bobber began jumping up and down. These talks about Daniel always got my nephews going. Martha and Chris had gone up to Massillon to see their friend Daniel who had lost his mind.

Daniel had been engaged to Chris's cousin Elizabeth, but the marriage had been broken off the last night before the wedding. It wasn't because of anything bad or dangerous Daniel had done, but because the people said he was getting stranger than a loon.

He used to play guitar and sing a lot with Chris when they were younger and they were good friends, but then he put away the music, and seemed to have a world all by himself inside of him. Two days before the wedding he just walked around the woods all day while the rest of the men were chopping wood.

Anyway, Matthew wanted to stay on the subject and he turned to me. "Wayne, how do you know if you're going crazy?"

I didn't want to say anything right away. "Ja, Wayne," said Aden. "You knew Daniel too. How do we know if we're going to become like him?"

"Vell, I think people usually don't know about it if they're going crazy. If you ask about it, you're all right." But that wasn't quite right either, and I knew that that wouldn't satisfy them either, so I said, "I've felt like I was going crazy too."

"Really, you did!" several of them said it.

"Ja, one time in my last year at school I had a problem of thinking, and my head felt like it was going to divide. It started with just a little thing with Smith. Vell, I think now it was little—it wasn't then. I thought Smith was so against me because I couldn't play on the pony league team that spring and he was the coach. I imagined playing and running away from home and all kinds of things and woke up at night and couldn't sleep. I thought sure I was going nuts."

"What did you do?"

"I went out and worked. It was spring and I worked in the fields, and did it as hard as I could. Ja, I plowed two acres a day for five days and missed a whole week of school. By the time you sweat and see what you have done in a day and then a week, you feel better and everything looks different."

I looked out across the blue pond and saw the fields on the other side. "The dirt would roll over and I kicked it with my toes. I talked to the horses and we got tired together. '*Ja*, Bob and Bill, we can finish this field today,' I said."

Aden interrupted me, "I can see how Grandpa was happy with you for that."

I cast my line and kept on. "Happy as a lark and I was too. In the evening I was as tired as the horses. It was as if the bad thoughts were dripping out of my skin and laying out on the field. I'm not saying everything got better right then, but it was a start. I could see that Smith wasn't against me, but he just wanted to have a good team. I could see why Ben couldn't just let me join a baseball team like that. I saw there were other things in life besides baseball and Smith. I began to see the whole picture."

The boys were quiet. I think they were a little surprised by what I told them. Finally Aden turned over to Matthew, "So you see what I told you. It isn't in the breeding and you can do something about it."

Vell, we kept on fishing and talking like that till we heard the glasspacks. We all looked over at the road, and there was the blue and white '55 Chevy with fender skirts and a coon tail swinging from the aerial. The *Buwe* shouted "Under!" and the car pulled up the little drive to the pond.

Quite a spiffy car Roy had. It was fixed up so that the front end pointed up in the sky and the back was down low, almost touching the ground. The car really looked streamlined with an airplane bird ornament on the hood.

That was it for fishing and going crazy for the boys. They wanted to see Roy, and we headed over to the diving board to see what was up.

The motor kind of up-chucked in an important way as the car slowed down. Through the open windows I could hear Gentleman Jim Reeves sing a song about love life in the West. Roy shifted down to low and came right up on the spillway of the pond. When he came behind the diving board, he gave it a final roar so that when he went off the gas, it popped like a row of firecrackers on the Fourth of July. Finally it toned down to a soft purr. Roy shut off the motor, but he kept the switch on and Gentleman Jim's music kept on coming.

"*Har Buwe.*"

Everybody just kind of nodded and then Joni, one of the Hershberger boys, said, "What brings you to these parts?"

"Are you really Roy?" asked another one.

"Who else did you think I was?" Roy answered.

"*Vell,* your hair are really cut different."

"Ducktail, that's what we all have now."

We just shrugged our shoulders.

"That's right, a duckass, latest style, and you'd better believe it."

Some laughed and others were putting their shorts on as Roy explained about the latest hairstyles. Judas, I'd heard this haircut story a hundred times, but we all listened closely. Roy was interesting, we all thought, and still I wasn't sure about him either. For the rest he was just an Amish boy who had gone wild, but for me he was my brother who caused much pain to the family.

He had left home when he was 18 and enlisted in the Army. He had a short strong body of muscle and bone on top of which he carried a small head with a short bull neck. He was strong and *litterlich,* and we were amazed at his strength and recklessness. I think the *Buwe* admired him for his backbone to get out of here and see the world. At the same time we pitied him for his lostness. He had a scar a little above his cheek that made him look especially old and tired, even if he was only 22. With his short neck, he looked a little like a young Hereford bull who had a good body, but had too many scars for his age. So he looked older than he really was.

There were all kinds of stories going around about Roy's strength, his women and his troubles. Nobody could do so much or so little. I should have known more about him because he was my brother, but I didn't. Sometimes — like now — he didn't even seem like my brother. He might as well have been some *Englischer.*

Anyway, he always looked for the *Buwe* when he came back on furlough. Most of the men his own age were getting married and having their own families. I even heard that Roy had a wife and child, but we never talked about it. But Judas, to me he was still a wild young boy and, anyway, where ever the *Buwe* were, Roy would soon find them. Then he'd tell them about his latest adventures with the Army or the cops — the fuzz — the way he called them.

"*Har Rotznees.* Hi snot-noses," he greeted the Yoder boys when he picked out his little nephews. "Are you catching any bullfrogs or minnows?"

"Bluegills and bass," they answered softly, a little afraid. But I could see that they also admired their uncle who came from strange countries and places. I felt like a pile of manure because I'd never been any place but Wooster and the Cleveland Zoo, and I wanted my nephews to admire me too.

"That's minnows. You should see the marlin I've been catching down off the coast of Florida."

"Big, eh?"

"You better believe it. I've caught them at over 12 feet and 1,000 pounds. Big fish. Nothing to play with. Why some of those fish have come right through a boat with their long sharp noses." He threw a stone into the little pond. "Why, this isn't even fishing compared with what you can catch down there on the coast. You'd better believe it."

"Do a lot of fishing?"

"Every other weekend and sometimes in between. There's plenty of time to fish. See you guys think that all we do is march around all day and polish our guns, but we have a lot of things going on and time off. *Ja*, I'm off to the coast every other weekend, you'd better believe it."

I could have thrown up. *Ja*, Roy, tell us about your fishing, about your fast car and about your strength. Tell us how everything is better wherever you are out in the world and how you've been all over the place.

The boys were all standing around with their mouths hanging open and waiting for more, like stupid little robins waiting for worms.

"Are you stationed down in Florida now?" asked Aden.

"*Ja*, I'm down there at Cape Canaveral now since I'm hooked up with the Air Force." He made it sound as if it were as simple to move from one service to another as it is to cross the county line. "Got a two-month leave so I'm taking it easy.

"See, with the Russians sending up a Sputnik in '57, we can't just sit back and let them get ahead of us in space. That's the key to this country, the key to the future — space. You just listen to me. I'll betcha in 10 years we'll be flying around in space capsules, and soon we'll visit the moon or the other planets. That's one thing I'll say for Kennedy; he knows the future is with space."

"*Ja vell*, who's so interested in the moon anyway?" This was Simon, one of Gravey Ben's boys.

"I don't expect you to understand all these things. I had no idea what was going on in the world either until I left this hollow. But it's the truth, by gum, and you'd better believe it."

He got out some glossy pictures of the different rockets and showed them to us, naming each one like he had given them the names himself.

"That one is the Red Stone rocket that I saw take off last month.

You've never seen anything like the spitting, the sparks and the fire of that animal, vicious but smooth as can be in the air. You could hear her from five miles away, and you'd better believe it."

It sounded like a dragon to me. I looked over the faces of the *Buwe*. They were just waiting for more of this rocket and Air Force and fishing talk. They really went for his baloney. This time it was about rockets. The last time he was in Korea, and he told us about how the Koreans eat raw fish and how they're still jumping and flipping their tails when they put the fish in their mouths.

Ja, we found out all about small houses with paper-thin walls and chopsticks, and I knew the boys were waiting for the cop stories. He would tell us about his chases with the cops and how he ran around the roadblocks. If Roy's stories were true or just made up, I really don't know. They were probably a little of both, and for the *Buwe*, it really didn't matter. They liked and feared him. He had a car and went places.

He looked over at me after a while and said, "Come on, Wayne, bring those little ones. I'll take you home; you're not catching anything, and I want to stop in and see Martha and the old man."

We hopped in the car. The little boys and John jumped in the back seat and felt honored by the invitation. How many boys had a relative who had seen rockets shoot off in space and had such a powerful car?

"Come on, Roy, make'm fly." The *Buwe* outside called to him as the doors slammed shut.

Roy put the gas all the way down on the floor, several times in a kind of yes signal. He put the car in low and looked over at the *Buwe* as if he were an airplane pilot waiting for the take-off signal. One of the Hershbergers flipped up his middle finger and that was all we needed. The clutch came flying out, the gas went straight down on the floorboard and the car jerked forward throwing stones and dust into the pond and onto the field. A cloud of dust floated behind us, and we roared up the main road. When the car came to the blacktop, the back tires gave a sharp squeal, and we squealed again when he shifted into second gear. Like I said, it was a pretty spiffy car.

"How do you like that power?" Roy looked over at me.

"Pretty good," I grunted. The three nephews were all sitting at the front edge of the back seat, clutching our seat and taking it all in. John sat up too, but he once told me he thought Roy was a rearend, and I think he still believed it.

In the next valley we came to a buggy moving along slowly and hanging to one side slightly. I could tell from the horse that it was Gravey Ben, our bishop. Roy tooted the horn loudly and the buggy moved to the side.

"There should be a law against those things, to keep them off the road," Roy snorted. "You'd better believe it. No where else in this country do you have the natives going around with these hazards."

None of us said a word. The Yoder boys only looked straight ahead and I looked back at Gravey and caught a glimpse of his face. I knew it wasn't right, and I thought of just this morning when Toots Hacker had passed me in the buggy. Gravey's eyes didn't look up at all. *Ja*, the world is bad, Gravey. Here we go. Take a look.

"Are Martha and the old man around home today?" asked Roy.

"No."

"Where are they?"

"They went to Massillon to see Daniel."

"The crazy."

"*Ja.*"

"If that guy would have had any sense at all he would have left here a long time ago, and he'd be alright. But he stayed here too long and where is he now? In the nuthouse, where else. Do you see what I mean? He hung around too long and you'd better believe it."

"*Ja.*"

"That's what happens when you've got something and you only stay here in the sticks."

"*Ja.*"

"So you little peewees remember that when you grow up." Roy stepped on the gas and the trees flew past us like ninety. We went through the woods where the tree branches came out and covered the road so that it's like you're going through a long covered bridge. It was my favorite place to drive with Flecha, but now it was gone so quickly it might as well not have been there.

"How about you?" He was talking to me.

"What do you mean?"

"Just that. When are you going to get out of this place?"

"Why do I have to?" Actually I sometimes wanted to, but I wanted to disagree with him when he talked like this. "There are others in the nuthouse. Only Daniel is from around here."

"You still going regular with that Hostetler girl?"

"*Ja.*"

"*Ja vell*, that explains it all. You'll never see anything as long as you're tied to a woman's cap strings. You'll never even know what else is happening. Vegetables don't know there's life outside the garden, unless some one cuts them off and throws them out or eats them. That's right and you'd better believe it."

Roy looked right at me and said, "You ought to get out, still. You should see some other parts of the world. You're smart and you get along with people. Really, if it weren't for that woman, you could leave and try something else." I really think he was trying to be nice, and I wanted to answer him to say that I had been thinking of the same thing, but then Aden jumped in.

"Did you hear how the *Buwe* hit one of the drakes again last night?" he asked.

"*Ja*, I was a part of it," I said.

The boys laughed. "It was really something. Boy, was Dad mad. He had to get up and help butcher the drake. So you were a part of it." They laughed some more. "He said that as far as he's concerned, the *Buwe* should have hit the whole *kitenkabutal* and stuck the feathers up their rearends."

"*Ja*, but the real thing was that he didn't want to get up early in the morning and dress them," said Raymond.

"The problem is with the buggies," said Roy. "If you would use cars you could toot your horn and scare the crap out of them. That would clear the lane."

Just then we came to the Yoder place near Holmesburg and there were the ducks. Roy tooted his horn and now he added a little musical tune at the end of it. The glasspack mufflers popped and cracked, the horn tooted some more and the ducks hissed and waddled off the driveway.

3.

Early the next morning I was out in the field mowing hay.
Red-winged blackbirds scolded and moved close to their nests as
the rattling mower moved along. Here and there a rabbit jumped
out. Lucky, I thought, that I hadn't cut off any legs.

It's the worst thing about mowing. These cottontails have no
brains about the danger of a mower, and they just sit there until you
cut off their legs. I hate it. Even worse is to cut off the legs of a
ring-necked pheasant. Not because they are better, even if they
look so nice, but because there just aren't so many.

After several rounds, I stopped for a break for the horses and to
grease. I looked over to the buildings and saw the '55 Chevy parked
beside the machine shed. That car was a sign of everything that
was wrong with my brother. No wonder the church didn't allow
them. Last night when we got back from Chris and Martha's, Roy
had soon left and got back who knows when this morning. And
who knows where he had been. That was just it, no control.

I probably could have asked him, but I didn't. He would have
thought I was meddling. Anyway, he thought I was some back-40
hayseed who was way too tied to a girl and my parents. And I know
I didn't always have the best thoughts about him either.

Part of it had to do with the man who came out of the barn and toward me. It was my father. He came down the lane and then turned up the field across the fresh alfalfa stems. I waited for him and watched him walk in his steady and forceful way. Ben was a strong man for his 60 years. The hat was tilted back a little, and his hairline could be seen in front under the brim. His face looked pretty red and his eyes were bright, even in their dark brownness.

I know some outsiders thought my father was cocky and rough, but I thought he was forceful and busy. Some of the people who didn't like him called him tight and stingy and self-willed.

He was mad. I could tell from way off by the way he regularly moved his right arm sharply to the front and stroked his scrubby beard. Every now and then he would kick at something on the ground, even if there was nothing to kick at.

I greased and oiled the mower, and then I heard him kick the scythe when he got close to us. "It's getting a little dry, isn't it?" he said.

"*Ja*, I oil it every several rounds," I said.

I put the oil can in the holder, and then my father stepped in front of me. He put his right hand up sharply and pulled his beard. "He's *litterlich*." That's what he always called someone who was wild and didn't follow our people's customs and beliefs.

I just grunted.

"No respect for his elders."

"Huh."

"I can't understand it," he said.

"Nope, I can't either."

"We left him get his own way too often."

"Huh."

"*Ja*, I thought it was just childishness."

I spit on the ground.

"Thought he would grow out of it."

"*Ja*, maybe he will."

"*Naw*, that's just the way *die Memm* thinks," he said. "He's *litterlich* and when you live that way for long, you just keep on living that way."

"Huh."

"We just left him go when he was little. Remember when he hid behind the barn during milking and how he'd throw stones at buggies from behind the weeping willow trees. We thought it was cute. As long as only Roy did it, it was all right. Do you remember that still?"

"*Ja,*" I said sadly. "I do."

"Never did like to work."

"Not here on the farm anyway."

"He'll never amount to anything."

"Uh-huh."

"Rebellious."

"I guess."

"How did he get like this?"

I only looked down at the freshly cut stubble. How the alfalfa smelled good. Then I looked up toward the shed and the car was moving. The glasspacks roared, and Roy was leaving. The car picked up speed as it flew down the lane, leaving a cloud of dust to settle over our farm. It was my brother's last blessing, shaking the dust off his car. I waved to him, but I don't think he saw me.

"*Vell,* there he goes," I said.

"Just as well," said Ben.

"Huh?"

"He still wants to get his own way. Saturday night he broke into the cellar and stole our wine. This morning he came up to me and wanted 200 dollars to buy another car. Judas River, he already owes me half of his inheritance. Then to come and ask for more money!"

"*Ja.*"

"You know as well as I do. He could have it if he worked for it. I told him that just a few minutes ago. And what does he do?"

I looked down the road, but I couldn't see the '55 Chevy anymore.

"He got mad, called me tight and said he's packing up and leaving for good. He'll never amount to anything."

"*Ja,*" I said as I chewed on an alfalfa stem. "We'll see."

"We'll see my foot. We know!" exclaimed my father. "Mind you, we know. Never amount to a thing."

He turned around and headed back to the buildings and I could hear him saying "*Litterlich*" to himself as he left. I got back on the mower and clicked to the horses. The red-winged blackbirds fluttered around their nests, and the grasshoppers jumped in rhythm in front of the scythe.

The sun climbed up to the middle of the sky as we went around the field. Large dark spots showed up on Bill and Bob where the sweat spread on their hides. Small and big flies landed on their skin, and their strong tails swished them away.

A big horsefly landed on Bill's rump and stuck. Bill swished at it, but it stayed and I slapped at it with the reins. The fly flew off to the side, circled around like an airplane and then landed at a different spot. A small drop of blood showed up where it had been earlier.

I pulled in the reins and stopped the team. Bill stomped his rear foot sharply trying to get rid of the horsefly sucking blood. I moved behind Bill and said softly, "Whoa Bill, whoa . . ."

Then taking off my hat I struck the fly with the brim, and it rolled off the wet rump. My, I hated those flies, the way they sucked blood to get their food.

Back on the seat, I clicked my tongue, and the team pulled forward again as we moved around the field. The mower vibrated and the metal seat jittered my body all over. My jaw felt loose, and my arm joints seemed to let go. I felt as if my arms and legs would fall off from the shaking. I felt *duddlich.* My hat vibrated down to my eyes until it got too low. Then I pushed it up and rumpled my damp hair. Soon it slowly settled down again until it got too low for me to see. Then I'd push it up again.

I chewed on some timothy stems and smelled the fresh alfalfa still damp at the bottom. The tops were now dry from the hot sun. High overhead I saw a small dot as a red-tailed hawk circled, gliding in the air currents.

Bounce came running across the field with a ground hog in his mouth. With his head high and his short tail up, he really looked important as he moved across the swath of cut hay. When he came to where the hay was standing, he put the ground hog down and lay down behind it. Spreading his two front paws on either side of it, he waited for me. His short stub tail moved right on time from one side to another.

My hunter, my wild hunter. Sometimes he went away for several days, but he always came back one morning, greeting everyone from his bare spot in front of the porch. It was like he owned our farm and had to come back to see that everything was in good shape — to greet us.

Bounce's red tongue was lolling from the mouth as big drops fell on the cut hay. His fur was wet and a few ticks were sticking to his legs. He stretched his back legs straight out behind him. He was the niftiest dog I'd ever seen. I tickled his loose skin on top of his head.

"So you came back to civilization. Huh. Good dog, Bounce," I said to him.

Bounce did not get up, but greeted me by giving his stub several more turns. I pushed the ground hog to the side with my toe. *"Vell,* there's one less of you varmints to dig holes in our field," I said. "Good dog, Bounce."

Bounce just turned his tail faster and looked straight ahead. Water dripped from his tongue and the hinges of his mouth.

"Smart animals, these ground hogs. But not smart enough for you." I rubbed his muzzle. "Now leave him out here in the field where the buzzards can take care of him. These things stink like everything." I took the dead animal by the tail and threw it over across the cut hay.

I started mowing again and Bounce ran along behind. At the end of the row, I unhitched the team and headed across the field. Bounce walked along behind, his tongue still lolling and water dripping.

At the barn I watered the horses and put them in their stalls. When I passed Flecha and her colt, she whinnied softly.

"Okay you lazy little girl," I said. "You'll get some oats too, but it's not that you deserve it. What did you do to earn your keep?" But she was my queen so I fed her anyway. She was my dating horse, my going-to-town horse, my church horse and my friend— even if she didn't pull like the work horses. As I left the stalls, I patted the big broad rumps of Bill and Bob, and at the sliding door in front of the barn I looked around one last time at the team. They were rumbling and crunching on oats. Hard workers all. Then I went to lunch.

We didn't say anything at lunch about Roy leaving or about Ben being gone, but Leona's face told us the story. Leona's eyes and thin nose were like a weather vane for the family feelings, and today the arrow pointed to pain. When these things happened she was especially nice and for my balogna, she brought me some maple syrup which *die Memm* always said I really didn't need.

The only one who talked about Roy was Benny. "*Schtadt geh*, going to town," he said. But he wasn't quite all there and liked to go to town, and he always said it for several days when someone else went to town. "*Schtadt geh.*" It was all we heard.

After lunch I lay down on the couch and looked at the *Farm Journal* for several minutes until I fell into a bad snooze. I usually caught a nap after lunch for about a half hour but not that day. I could only think of Roy and that wasn't rest.

I opened my eyes and there sat my sister. I thought I was dreaming, but there she was rocking away. Leona sat still as a stone and looking straight ahead. I looked at her for a while, and I could see that she was in pain. Leona often felt the pain of our family. It was as if she carried the problems of our family in her large gentle face. Today it was sad.

"You shouldn't give up hope," she said.

But I blurted out, "Where did he go? How does he feel that he can leave us just like that and let the family go? Does he believe in anything?"

Leona didn't say anything right away. Her thin arrow of a nose moved slightly with her breathing on her large sad face.

"Dad went to town," she finally said.

"Will he write him out of the will?" I said the hated words. "He told me the last time Roy left home that he'd write him out if Roy didn't repent. Why does my father hate his son so?"

"Maybe he doesn't," she said.

"Then why is he so strict? Can't he bend just a little? Sometimes when you do what's right you just make it worse. When Roy finds out about the will, Judas, that will be the end."

"You don't know that he wrote him out of the will," she said.

"Do you?" I asked.

"No." She kept on rocking.

I looked closely at my sister and knew that women could do these things better. They knew how to take these things in stride.

"Why can't Roy be like Anna?" I said. "She isn't tame either, but she doesn't go against the church and her parents. Why can't he live peaceably when he's home?"

Leona smiled and *die Memm* came in the room, and I knew our talking was over.

I got up and Leona looked at me. She smiled on her face, but deep down in her heart she was sad at the same time. She was the only person I ever knew who could do that and it wasn't just put on. I think that's why I could tell her things.

The team whinnied softly to welcome me when I came back to the barn. Bounce and I followed the horses down the lane, and they were as eager as I was to get back to the mowing. The sun was up high and everything was dry now. On our first round, Bounce stopped to sniff the ground hog he had caught that morning. The belly had already swollen and the eyes had a shiny glazed look. Bounce stood in front of it, scratched a little dirt on it, and then he left for the back-40.

I smiled as I watched him go. I even wished I could go with him. He stayed around the farm like the other animals, but then he took off on expeditions. Bill McCollough once claimed that he had spotted him near Wooster. That's 12 miles away, but he always came back. We used to joke that Bounce was in the Army and came back on furlough, but that was before Roy joined the Army. Now it wasn't funny any more.

I sometimes wondered if I could have a wild spirit like Bounce. He left and was wild, and he came home and we never knew that he had been away. He fit in wherever he was. But people didn't act like that.

Bounce never talked one thing about his trips. That was his business. We didn't ask him questions; he didn't ask us. But when he came home, he knew what was expected of him. He did enough of that to get along. He knew that Holmesburg was one place and the world was another, and he didn't try to change them. But people were different.

Maybe it was better that Roy left and didn't get along here. He had joined the world, and so you didn't expect him to get along with us. Still he was my brother, and I wished he would come back. Gravey Ben did. We shouldn't give up hope, Leona had said and she was right.

Anna could do it best. I liked to think of Anna, not as a wild one, yet she really was. She went to carnivals, and when a ride was up to go to a concert in Wheeling, she went. She never let that get in the way of her being right with the family and the church. She dressed prim and spiffy, but in the *Attnung* of the church. At church meetings on Sundays she didn't test the *Attnung* or get people mad. She didn't sing another part of the hymn the way Chris once did. Crazy man tried to sing tenor one Sunday morning. Only my brother-in-law Chris would try a half-baked trick like that. She didn't wear a cap with fewer pleats like that Hershberger girl did. Nope, she knew the *Attnung*.

But not Roy. When he left us he wanted to come back and wreck our family. He tried to make us feel bad about our life, like it wasn't important. I couldn't answer for him, but you shouldn't do everything against the tradition.

The mower rattled and my jaw dropped . My eyes moved from the line of the hay cutting to the broad strong rumps of the team. My jaws and arms and legs were falling off again, and I was all *duddlich*.

A poor rabbit's squeal brought me back to the mowing. "Ach, I was hoping I would miss them today," I said to myself. If I had cut only one leg, it might have survived, but with two gone, it couldn't move. I picked up the screaming bunny and gave the neck a twist, ending the misery. I threw the warm body into the hay where the buzzards would find it.

I stopped and watched some of the crows come to the freshly cut hay. A scout came ahead of the flock and looked out over the field, and he must have thought I was safe. Soon he gave a signal and the whole flock landed while the sentinel flew back to the lone dead tree.

By mid-afternoon we were finished. The sun had moved to the western side of the sky. The horses were wet all over, but they were eager to keep on going. They trotted, and I had to hold them back as we headed for the barn and some oats. Every now and then I would look back over my shoulders at the freshly cut field. I hoped it wouldn't rain. The hay would make good feed for the winter.

That evening Ben was back and talked just like usual, and it seemed as if nothing had happened. I went to bed early and looked at Roy's bed. It was the same bed he had slept in since he was a little boy. The room was cleaned up now, but Roy was gone. I sat on the bed for several minutes and softly pushed myself up and down on the springs.

Outside I heard the crows squawking as they were gathering on the dead oak tree on the back-40. I took off my clothes and looked out the window. Maybe I should head for the back-40 too, I thought. Then my eyes turned to the field of hay we had cut that day. I could smell the fresh alfalfa through the open window. The crows called for a long time that evening and I lay down. But a long time passed before I could go to sleep.

4.

We got a surprise visitor. I just came out of the barn the next afternoon when a blue car drove up the lane with Ben sitting in front and an *Englischer* driving. What is this? I thought. My father goes to Millersville and loses a son and picks up an *Englischer* in return. The next thing my good father buys a tractor and joins the Conservatives. *Ja*, and Bounce will bring home one of his English collies, the Russians and Americans will become friends and Anna will go on a grape diet.

The car stopped in the drive between the house and barn, and Ben and the young man got out. For once my father Ben didn't seem to be in charge of everything. He acted as if he didn't know what to do right away. He just got out of the car and watched the *Englischer* and I did too.

The fellow was about my own age. He looked me straight in the eyes and we shook hands. You may not be too sure of yourself, but you are sincere, I thought. His brown eyes were soft and friendly. He had red hair and freckles on his face, but he was still pretty grown-up. His clothes were a plain cotton light yellow shirt, and the pants were wrinkled but not dirty.

I'll have to admit that I liked him right away. It wasn't so much for what he said as for what he didn't say. Most of the *Englischer* who we met like the McColloughs thought they were a lot better than we were, or they were riffraff like Toots Hacker, or they were bankers or lawyers who we met in town.

Benny came dashing out of the barn swinging the ropes he had around when he was playing horse and team. *"Schtadt geh,"* he said running up to the young man. *"Schtadt geh,"* he barked like a puppy, but it got us to talking.

He shook hands with the *Englischer* who finally said, "My name is Malcolm Smith. I'm from Philadelphia."

I gave him my hand too. "I'm Wayne Weaver. I live here and this is my brother Benny." I didn't tell him that Benny wasn't quite all there, and anyway, we can't change how many brains God gave us. Benny came up to him and pumped his hand again.

Then my father's tongue let loose in *Deitsch.* "I met him in Millersville. He wants to live with us. What do you think?"

I looked over at Malcolm. "You like it here?"

"This is beautiful countryside. I came down Route 76 from the north, and soon I was in these hills and small farmsteads. The wheat shocks are placed in the fields in the most symmetrical patterns." That's the way he talked and I knew he was educated. "I had heard about Holmes County, but this is my first time to drive into the area."

"Isn't Philadelphia in the east?"

"Yes, but I'm a student at Hanna Northern University in Cleveland, and I drove from there. I was doing some studies this summer."

"He wants to live with us," said Ben again in *Deitsch.* "I think he has some brains, and he's not a rearend the way many of these city slickers are."

I wanted to tell my father to be quiet. What if he understood some *Deitsch.* Did he have to be so rude? I tried to make up to the stranger.

"So you're a college student, eh?" I asked.

"Yes, I was in a sociology course this spring and we were studying about the Amish people. I visited their settlement near Philadelphia."

"Lancaster, *ja,*" I said. "I know about Lancaster. That's over in *Pennsylvany.*"

"Well, I visited there last year and they said there were even more Amish out in Ohio."

"Vell, here in Holmesburg, we're at the northern edge of the

settlement. If you really want to see the middle of it you have to go east of Millersville to around Breman and down to Charm. Around Putsch, there it gets pretty thick." I thought of Anna. She was right in the middle.

"Why don't we take him over to Chris's tonight? He wants to know about our living and beliefs and Chris can say more." Ben then switched to English. "*Ja*, we'll take you over to Chris, my son-in-law, tonight. But now I've got to work." Ben turned around and headed toward the barn. He scratched his head as he went. *Vell* good, he wasn't mad and the young man was decent.

So that evening after dinner, Ben, John and I piled in the blue Plymouth with Malcolm and went to visit Chris and Martha. Chris invited us all in the living room, and then he told Malcolm all about life on the farm and about our beliefs. Even I learned a lot. That Chris knows a lot about these things even if he isn't that good a farmer.

He went deep in the history and told about the Anabaptist movement in the sixteenth century and how we're different from the Reformers and the Catholics. How he can remember all those names was something. He remembered more names than I ever forgot.

He got on Jacob Amman and our break away from the Mennonites. He said the right year and had other things about people like Menno Simons and Dietrich Philips and other people I'd never heard of.

Chris could really get interested in talking about our history, and this Malcolm actually knew what he was talking about. I could tell by the way they asked each other good questions, and they seemed to know about the names.

Malcolm was most interested in our life today, and he already knew about districts and ministers. Chris told him there are about 44 districts in our settlement and that each district has about 40 families and a deacon, two ministers and a bishop.

Chris finally showed him our martyr books. I knew something about these, and the pictures I'll never forget. Chris had the real one — our *Martyrs Mirror* — and then he had an English one called *Fox's Book of Martyrs*. He said he'd give them to Malcolm to read.

"See that little drawing there," he said pointing to the first page of the *Martyrs Mirror*. "*Arbeite und Hofe*, work and hope. That is our people. We work and hope, trusting the mercy of the good God to take care of us. See that little man with the shovel."

Malcolm looked closely at the little drawing of a farmer digging into the dirt, a small bird and a house in the back.

"But that is our problem too; we try to work too hard and some of our people don't have assurance of salvation. We try to work our way to heaven and forget that we can know we'll get there only by grace through faith." I should have known this was coming. Chris then stopped and looked at my father. Ben was looking at a hole in the floor and rubbing his elbow. *Ja*, Chris you go into these things, and you're in hot water.

This was Chris's ax to grind, and we could all see it coming. If we would just believe and say things like the Baptists or the Mennonite revival preachers, or whatever other riffraff. Then we'd have Jesus in our hearts, and we'd all be alright.

My father didn't get into an argument on that — especially here in public — but I knew where he stood. He once told me that it's all well and good to say these things, but if you took them too far or make them an ax to grind, you weren't Amish anymore and Chris had better be careful.

Chris coughed. He looked at Martha who was holding little Samuel and looking right down at the floor too. *Ja*, Martha, you are right in the center of the room. Chris looked around the room and all at once he knew that if he kept on that way, he'd be all alone. If we had to choose between his way of talking and Ben and the church, we knew who would win, hands down.

"*Vell*, I don't need to go into all of that, but that picture tells you a lot about us. We work the soil, build up our homes — see that little house back there — and we trust God."

Malcolm paged through the book stopping at some of the terrible pictures of people being burned at the stake. He couldn't read any of the German, but the pictures were enough.

"We have been a suffering people," Chris said. "Both the Catholics and Protestants turned on us and a lot of blood was shed. This book tells all about the many cases. You'd think that if people didn't fight back and lived the way Jesus Christ taught, they would be exterminated like we kill pigeons. But somehow we survived. God takes care of his own."

Malcolm then all at once got interested in the women. He turned to Martha and asked, "Were the women also active as religious leaders?"

"I think so," she said.

"What is the main part of being Amish to you?"

"The family." She said it just like that and then she looked away. Little Samuel clung to her neck. My sister had not said anything during this time, and she wasn't interested in telling this man more than he actually asked. He could ask Chris. Her husband liked to talk.

"When will he go home?" Samuel said loudly in *Deitsch* to Martha. His older brothers giggled and Martha shushed him. Chris quickly led us out to the front yard.

The rest of the evening the three older boys, my nephews, stood right in front of the stranger and tried to figure out what kind of man he was. I was too. He was educated all right, but he wasn't like one of our school teachers. It was almost as if he were interested in everything, but still he didn't want to push his way around.

"Would you like to see our rabbits?" the boys asked. They were just waiting for this so they could show off their projects. Ben said he wanted to talk to Chris and Martha a little so we went off with the boys to see their projects. They had rabbits, bantys, ducks, guineas and what have you, all with their own names. They told everything from prices to trading them to the fights the banty rooster had with the dark Cornish rooster. I couldn't figure out why Malcolm was interested in any of it, but he listened to them.

Raymond showed us a little motor that he had bought, and how he had plans all made to build a tractor with gears and everything. I don't like to say proud, but I thought pretty good of my little nephews. Clever little fellows that they are.

Oh and did they ever have the questions. Did he have any brothers and sisters? How big is Philadelphia? How many times bigger than Wooster? Like Cleveland? But not as big as New York or Tokyo or London? Which sports did he play? Hunting, softball or basketball? Did he ever see the Indians play in Cleveland? No. Well, they have some good hitters: Franconia and Piersall. He didn't know about them? *Ja*, they're good.

Isn't the Liberty Bell still in Philadelphia? He saw it, eh? No, but it is a big bell and it's cracked. That's where Ben Franklin and William Penn lived, the city of brotherly love. Did he ever wish he had brothers and sisters?

That's the way these little ones were, always asking questions. My father didn't think it was all good. Chris and Martha let those little ones have too much rope, and if they're not careful they can hang themselves. That's what we did with Roy, he once told me.

We went from Philadelphia to Washington and to who knows where else and came back to the projects and how much the rabbits were bringing at the Fredricksburg sale. Then Ben and Chris came back to us.

Malcolm then asked them right out if he could hire himself out to be a farmer for the rest of the summer.

Ben asked him about his parents and then he wanted to know more of why he wanted to live here. "Are you sure you want to live with us?" asked Chris.

"I think so."

"But why? Are you just curious?"

"Yes, but more than in a superficial way." I later noticed that he often used the word *superficial*. He thought most people looked at things just from the outside.

"We don't like to be studied by people who don't believe," said Chris.

"But I do believe. I'm looking for other ways to live."

"*Ja vell*, we can always try it," said Chris. "But you would have a hard time becoming one of us."

"I agree."

"What kind of work would you like to do?"

"Farm work."

"Have you done it before?"

"No."

My nephews and John giggled, and we gave them some eyes that let them know that that was enough.

We talked a little more in *Deitsch*, and we decided that it was alright even if it was kind of a half-baked idea. Ben said he was interested in seeing if he would work.

"Tell you what," said Chris. "Would you like to live where there are other young people your age?"

"That would be fine."

So we talked some more by ourselves, and we decided it would be best for him to be at our place for a few days, even if the little boys wanted to have him at Chris's. We had more room, more work and more young people his own age.

I could tell that my nephews and John were all disappointed about this because the nephews had wanted to pump him with more questions. John, on the other hand, saw him as just another tramp.

"*Ja vell*, I wouldn't know why you couldn't come with us," said Ben.

"Well, I would like that very much," said Malcolm.

My father cleared his throat. "Just like to make sure we understand a few things."

"Huh? Yes, that would be helpful."

"No smoking in or around the buildings."

"I don't smoke."

"Even if you did, I don't allow it."

"Right."

"The car is to stay parked behind the machinery shed."

"I'll put it there."

"Third." Ben lifted his three fingers. "Around here everyone has to work. Now, if you go into a city, you'll see a lot of people standing around or just doing nothing. But around here we work."

Malcolm nodded his head.

"You're from the city aren't you?"

"Yes, Philadelphia."

"So you know what I'm talking about. *Vell*, here it's different."

For my father the world was divided into *die faul* and *die hatscaffich*, the lazy and the hardworkers. Many people work because they have to, but our people work because they want to. Ben used to say that it was the difference between a horse who pulls against the reins and one who has to be driven with a whip.

Actually, my father had thought this out some, and he once told me that's why he didn't want his children to ever have to work in a factory. He said that in farming or building or a trade, we work because we're doing something important and useful for the neighbor or ourselves. In a factory people don't like their work, and they are only doing it for the money. That's not good.

Chris went to the house and came back with the martyr books. "Take your time with these books and give them back when you're finished."

When we got back home it was dark and Leona, Benny and *die Memm* were on the porch. We told them our plans and after Benny shook hands for the twentieth time, it was off to bed. I thought of Roy as Malcolm got into my brother's bed. Where was he tonight and why couldn't he be decent like this *Englischer?* But I was sleepy and that was about it until I heard the alarm go off in the morning.

I got up and had my shirt on when Malcolm said pretty sleepily, "What time is it?"

"Five-thirty."

"Is this the time you usually get up?"

"Yup, sometimes even earlier," I said as I finished my shoelaces and headed for the door. "I'm going out to the barn now. You can come too."

I caught a whiff of the bacon grease in the kitchen as I went through the door. Outside the air was fresh and everything seemed so close, it almost touched me: the buildings, the animals and the morning sun. I heard the animals and smelled the urine in the straw. It gave the air a sharp odor the way the bacon grease made the kitchen smell good.

Ben, Leona and John were already scattered under the cows in the barn when I got my pail. Benny was trying to make a kitten stay on top of Bounce's back. I looked over these people who were so close to me. It was one of those times when you feel you're in unity with everyone else and the world. I liked them. Maybe it was the stranger in the house last night that all at once reminded me how much *die Memm* and these people under these cows and this nitwit brother with the cats was a part of me and always would be in a way I'd never be to others.

Malcolm came up to the door, panting and hurried.

"You decided to join us," I said.

"I'm here," he said.

"Grab a pail and you can work on that one down at the end of the line," I said. I helped him get started on Sally who was almost dry and didn't give much milk. Sally was gentle and good for practice. I showed him how you begin with priming, and then go with some steady pumping and on to the final drawing out. Our cows were all pretty gentle and only Daisy was nervous because she had a calf.

"Why do you call them all English names?" he asked me. "There's Alice, Star, Wanda, May, Daisy and Brindle."

"Because those are good cow names," I said. But I never thought of it just like that before. Wonder what he expected? Should we call them Mandy, Elizabeth, Katie, Sarah, Ruth and Anna? Judas no, those are people's names.

After the chores, we went in and Dad read the morning prayers as we knelt down. I smelled the bacon and thanked God for the good food.

It was good, and *die Memm* had eggs and toast and honey and applesauce too. It was something to see Malcolm eat. And the nice way he talked about the breakfast and Sally, you would have thought Sally was a big milker who had given a pail and a half.

And he tried to say nice things to *die Memm*.

"Your eggs were excellent."

"Uh huh," she said.

"The honey was too. Was that some you produced here?"

"Uh huh." *Die Memm* left the table and brought him some cold cereal and milk. He ate that too. I got hungrier just watching him eat.

After breakfast my father scraped his chair back and put a toothpick in his mouth, and I knew he was going to make an announcement.

"Bert's coming by to pick me up to go to the Kidron Sale today," he said. "Think that hay will be ready to turn over?"

I looked over at Malcolm, "One of the important things in farming is going to sales. That's the father's job." Dagnabbit, that was my father, always going to sales when he wanted to.

"*Vell,* it's one of the things I have to do to know the prices."

"Yup, going to the sales and visiting with the neighbors keeps this farm going," I said again to Malcolm. I shouldn't have said it that way, but I did.

Ben continued, "That's right. I want to watch what the shoats are bringing and see if we want to sell this corn or feed them out before the fall."

Leona looked over at me, and I noticed that the weather was changing from sunny to cloudy. She got up and when she took my plate, she flicked my ear really hard. I knew all fathers could do that — just run off to sales — but it wasn't right to the children. Why couldn't he consider how we felt about it. We wanted to go sometimes too.

"Anyway when you get your own family and farm, you can decide if you want to go to a sale or not." Ben finished the discussion and stood up. "You can work on that hay today."

"We will."

"Take the *Englischer* with you but keep him out of danger," he said in *Deitsch.*

"Uh huh."

"Let him work."

"He wants to."

My father left the room.

5.

Bert Stutzman's big livestock truck stood in the driveway. It was clean and sleek and the motor hummed like a sewing machine. Bert kept his trucks in A-number-one shape and it seemed like the cows never pooped on his sideboards.

"Do you have another hired hand?" Bert greeted us.

"Naw, it's an *Englischer*," Ben said as he climbed in the cab for the Kidron Sale. *Ja,* Dad would explain it all to him on the way to the sale. That was his privilege to go to the sale because, *vell,* he was Dad. But he still shouldn't overdo it.

I watched my father and Bert head down the lane. I knew that this was a high point in my father's week. This was the gravy on the potatoes, the cream on the strawberries. He would see a lot of his friends and relatives and complain that the school levy might pass. On the way, he'd tell Bert how bad it is about the money wasted on high school sports. Bert would just nod his head even if he had a big boy at the high school and wished there'd be a bigger gym for him to play in.

I kept on thinking of my father's sale day like this and then Leona's little ear flick came back to me and just like that my madness went away. That Leona knew how to handle these things. I even thought it was funny—there goes the hard worker who knows everybody else is lazy for his day at the sale. I looked over at

John, Benny and Malcolm and came out of my little meditation.

"Come, boys, let's get the barn cleaned out. The way that sun is coming out, we'll soon have some hay to turn over."

We had to clean the milking stalls every morning. We swept the floor, cleaned the gutter and threw lime on the floor.

"How did that truck driver know how to speak *Deitsch?*" asked Malcolm.

"He's Mennonite."

"They speak *Deitsch?*"

"Some, those who were Amish," I said. "Their kids don't know it."

"So that's a Mennonite; an Amishman who went English."

"No, but a lot around here used to be Amish, especially the Conservatives," I said. "Actually, if you go back over 100 years maybe, we were all Amish Mennonites here in Holmes County. But then some splits came, so now you have all kinds. Chris could explain them better for you."

"Chris was telling me about them yesterday, but I have trouble keeping them all apart."

I didn't think I could explain it any better, but I tried anyway. "*Vell*, there are mainly the Amish and the Mennonites and then you have all kinds of groups in them. In the Amish you have the *Hinnereste*, that means the closest to the back. Some are called the Swartzentrubers, the Sam Yoders and there's the Tobe church."

"They're called after their leaders?" asked Malcolm.

"*Ja*, I think, and some call them bad names, but that's not right. They're all pretty strict."

A barn swallow flew in with a bug and gave it to her young nest full by one of the huge beams. Then swoosh and a sharp call and she was gone out the open door again.

"Now on the other side you have the Beachy Amish," I said. "They drive black cars and use tractors like the Mennonites, but otherwise they look like us. But these groups are pretty small. Most of the people are just plain Amish like us."

I scraped the manure through the gutter. "Here, you can try it," I said and gave it to him. But he kept on asking questions so I told him about the Mennonites, but that was harder because I didn't know as much about them.

"There are the main Mennonites like Bert Stutzman who drove in here. They would be like the main group of Amish. Then there are the Conservatives; they're also called the peewees. The main thing about them is that most of them left the Amish or the Beachys not too long ago. There are probably some other kinds too, but they all look the same to me. Chris could tell you more about that."

"Do they ever inspect the barn for sanitation?" asked Malcolm. I was glad he changed the subject.

"Naw, they never come," I said. "We send milk to the cheese house and they don't inspect. They just trust us to keep the place clean. Some people send to grade A places like Orrville, but there you have inspectors coming all the time. You need a milkhouse, a cooler and probably with time a set of milkers."

"But you have some of those things."

"*Ja, vell,* we have the milkhouse and the cooler, but some do not."

Benny brought a cat to Malcolm, and he was meowing like a real cat himself.

"Meow," said Malcolm. "Does it pay more if you send to a Grade A producer?"

"Oh *ja,* I believe they are getting about $4.50 per hundred, and we're getting $3.70 so there's almost a dollar difference." Benny kept right on meowing like a tom. "Anyway the cheese house is not far away so it's handy. And Dad helped to found it. He's been the treasurer for many years and so we have a part in it. We've always sent our milk there."

That seemed to satisfy him for a while so we worked on in silence.

"How do you decide whether to have milkers or not?"

"The whole district decides that."

"How does the group decide?"

"*Vell,* we talk about it for a while and then the ministers announce the decision at the *Attnung* meeting. There are a lot of things to consider, so it takes time."

"Does everyone agree then?"

"Pretty well, and if a few don't they'll go along with it to keep unity and the peace. Actually most of us don't need milkers right now. As long as we have plenty of hand milkers and send to the cheese house, we're all right."

"Do any people around here have milkers?"

"*Ja,* sure the Beachys do; they're almost Amish, but they use electric and so do the Mennonites, and of course the *Englische.*"

John butted in and said to me. "I think even some districts out in Indiana have milkers when they are driven on an engine."

"But not many," I said trying to get it right. "Ah look, the cows don't like that lime in the feed." I showed Malcolm not to throw the lime in the front of the stanchions.

"Yes, yes, we'll keep it in back with the gutter."

"John, you can start harnessing the mules anytime. Think I'll use them today," I said as we finished the gutter. *"Vell,* this is clean enough for Grade A."

"It even smells good."

"Yup, that lime kills the germs."

"Lots of these things," I said, thinking back on what we had said about the milkers, "are hard to explain and to understand. You just have to watch and you'll catch on."

"I'm trying," he said.

We hitched the mules to the rake, and I raked the hay which we had cut the other day. Malcolm, Benny and John fed the chickens and did some other things around the barn that I put them on.

After dinner the hay was dry and we were ready to load. We hitched Bill and Bob to the wagon and put the loader on back of the wagon. John drove, and I gave Malcolm a fork to load in the front. That was a mistake. I told him to stomp it down and to throw some in the corners, but he didn't know beans about using a pitchfork, and he threw off as much as he got in the corners. Anyway, he could have stuck one of us.

"Whoa," I called. "Look, I can make it. You just stomp when I need it. Two pitchforks on this wagon are too many."

The load kept on rising. The place for him to learn to use that fork was in the mow where he couldn't hurt anybody. Most of the time Malcolm stood beside John on the uprights. John was all eyes on his driving and paid no attention to the visitor.

I liked the haymaking. It took skill and hard work, and you knew the animals would appreciate it next winter. I threw the dry and sweet-smelling alfalfa and timothy to the front and layer by layer built an even load. In back I left it roll and just guided it to its place. Sometimes I'd walk to a corner to stomp it down, but slowly the hay rose. I pushed the loader chute up to the highest notch, and John and Malcolm climbed to the next to last uprights.

Beads of sweat began to show out from under the brim of my hat, and I could see some dark spots of sweat beside my suspenders. My blue chambray shirt was getting all dark from the wet. My crotch and my shorts were damp. The water seemed to make the work go easier. I steadily threw one forkful after another or rolled the hay toward the front, and it stayed even pretty nice. I lost track of Malcolm and John and the horses. All that mattered was the hay and the fork and myself as we went up together. It was as though

God had made us to be all part of one operation on top of that hay wagon on that hot day.

I could only see the heads of John and Malcolm in the front. "High enough," I called. The wagon was full.

"Whoa, Bob. Whoa, Bill," said John gently to the team.

"Nice hay," I said as we walked around the top stomping down the last layer of alfalfa. Ah, this is good food. No rain on it and it's dry and light. The cows will like it next winter. I pulled the rope to let go the loader and went to the front of the wagon. John gave me the reins.

"Didn't see any snakes did you?" Malcolm thought I was joking, but I wasn't. "Worst thing to get on a load like this is a black snake," I said. "Every now and then one of them gets on a load."

But I couldn't think of snakes long. Bill and Bob pulled on the lines to trot as our wagon headed back toward the barn. The chains of the harness jingled in time with their steps, and I felt just as new as my eager horses bumped softly down the field. We felt the breeze come over the wagon every now and then and it made the alfalfa smell sweeter and stronger. Even the whiff of Bounce's old dead ground hog didn't stay long.

Malcolm was breathing deeply with his eyes closed like some Hindu in meditation. *Vell,* maybe that's the way the Quakers pray. We never heard a peep from him all the way home. John looked at me and made his finger go in a circle by his head like he was out of his mind. I winked at him. Let the *Englischer* enjoy it. The sun was warm and the hay was just right.

I drove the team into the big doors on the second floor of the barn. We all had to help unload, but I had to kind of direct the operation from the top of the wagon since my father wasn't there.

Along the length of the barn's gable we had a track with grapple hooks attached by a rope tackle. I stuck the hooks into the load of hay and then Leona drove the mules away from the barn, and this lifted the big dump of hay with the rope. When the load got to the top, I yelled "Whoa" and Leona stopped the mules. A ratchet held the load while Leona hitched the mules to another rope and pulled the load sideways. When the load was in the place where we wanted it, John tripped it, and it came sailing down with a woosh of flying air and then settled on the mow with a plop.

I put Malcolm to helping John with the mowing. They attacked the pile and made it even on both sides. They were as different as night and day, and I began to see how much experience meant. John was only 16, but he knew exactly how to move the hay to the corners. He pushed if off the top and rolled it. Malcom's fork always skimmed off the top with only a few whisps, or else he sent it in real deep, and he couldn't lift it.

"Do you usually try to roll it or is it better to pick it apart?" he asked John.

"Doesn't make that much out," John said. "Sometimes one way works better, sometimes another, depends on the load. Just go with the hay. If a piece hangs together, sometimes you can roll a large piece to the side." John spit in the hay. He knew what he was talking about.

"What you don't want to do is try to get the hay underneath. The old man used to tell about this one fellow who was always trying to get the hay underneath the pile. '*Ja*, why don't you get the hay on top?' they'd ask him. '*Vell*, I can always get the top, but I want to get to the bottom.'"

John laughed and I thought it was funny too, even if I had heard it before. "That fellow didn't get much done. Nope. Didn't work with the grain."

"What does that mean?"

"You do what comes naturally. It comes from wood. The wood has a grain that goes in a direction. Now, if you sand the wood with the grain it's easy, but if you try to sand the wood across the grain, it gets all rough and nothing comes out right. You're doing it rearend backwards. I don't care what the book says. You can't always go by the book. You've got to do things the way they are from experience. Work with the grain."

John was really talking away. I think he felt so good in seeing how well he was doing in hay mowing and his farming experience that it went to his head a little, but Malcolm didn't seem to mind listening.

John tripped another load. The grapple hooks tingled loudly like bells as the hay flopped down and the hooks clanked together. Then John went on to another lecture.

"Good invention, those grapple hooks. Before them people used to use harpoons and slings to do this work. Dangerous, those harpoons. Only straight points coming down through the hay. The old man once told of a guy who got killed by one. The thing accidently let loose with a man underneath and it went right through him. Died like a seal on an ice block in the Arctic."

"That's a terrible way to die."

"*Schrecklich*, terrible," said John. "Come on over here," he said to some hay as he threw it into the corner. *Vell*, I was glad to see my brother work hard and taking on with our visitor. It was the first time he acted friendly like this, and I think it was the working together that did it.

Work brought us together. I felt it in the air the next few loads; it was the sweat, the crackling of the hay, the dust and the dim light of the mow with slices of sun coming in the barn doors. It's the same feeling I would get sometimes when we would all sing in church or when we would all stand close together at a sale and the auctioneer told a silly joke. Work brings you together like that. My father knew what he was talking about when he liked work. Work and hope.

I was hot and sweaty and my shirt was wet as a dish rag. I could feel every whiff of air that came through the big doors. Every now and then I looked down the front of my shirt and saw the water trickle against my belly. With my tongue I tasted the salty water on my upper lip. John had stopped his farm lectures, and there was just the sound of the ropes and pulleys and the grapple hooks.

Then all at once Malcolm said something: "This is the real life." He said it just like that.

"What was that?" asked John.

"Nothing," said Malcolm. Then he kind of stuttered out with, "Well, I said 'This is real good hay.'" But that's not what I had heard.

"Darn tootin'," said John. "The cows will be happy as larks this winter."

Before the next load Leona brought lemonade and we stood around chewing out the rinds and being entertained by Benny. It took work to get the rest of us together, but Benny was a friend to all of us all the time, even in talking. I think God saved him from some of the bad things our minds can do to the rest of us like being afraid, greedy and jealous.

"*Schtadt geh,*" he said as he spit the little pits of the oranges and lemons. He reached in and got a lemon rind for Malcolm. I don't think it made a thing out to him that Malcolm was an *Englischer.* He could have been purple or black or green or a Jew or a Greek for all Benny cared.

"Thank you," said Malcolm as he took the soaked rind. He looked over at Leona, "And tell your sister she makes good lemonade." Leona turned red and looked down, but I could read the weather and Leona's sun was still shining.

John and I headed back to the field. The alfalfa smelled sweet and the wagon bumped as it went over a ground hog hole. I dreamed of the future as I looked at the light blue clouds. Sometime I'd have my own hay field and ground hog holes. I might put out some clover too. Cows like it, and I wouldn't have to keep a field in it for several years in a row. *Ja*, I'll put out some alfalfa and clover and, of course, some timothy for roughage. I suppose Anna could drive the team sometimes when we get started. Or I could always get the Yoder nephews to help. Chris will give us one of them during the busy season.

Why did he want to do our work? Did he have a girlfriend too? Or was there something going on in the way he looked over at Leona? How long would he last here? But why worry, the work had brought us together. I looked back at the barn where Malcolm would be watching Benny kick pieces of hay around the floor or having the cats do tricks.

A pheasant hen and some little chicks ran ahead of us along the fence row.

6.

We went to bed early that evening. Haymaking took a lot out of us and I was tired. The bed felt good, and a nice breeze came in the window and went out into the hall. A large fly whirred at the window screen; it sounded like a chain saw a long ways off.

Even though I was tired, I felt clean and new from the swim we took at the Hershberger pond that evening. John, Benny, Malcolm and I had jumped in Malcolm's car and gone to the Hershbergers for a dip. Actually, it was John's idea, and I think that after working so hard with Malcolm, we all felt we wanted to do something together with the *Englischer*. But it didn't work out that way at the pond.

There were some other *Buwe* at the pond, and they weren't very friendly. It was my lesson number one in dealing with Malcolm, which I guess I never really learned. It was that you can get along with a stranger in the family where you know a little more who he is, but it's hard to have him mix with some who don't know him.

The *Buwe* only talked in *Deitsch* and asked me all kinds of questions, and most of them kept more clothes on. That's all except Benny and Simon Hershberger. Benny didn't know the difference, and Simon said he wasn't going to put on shorts just because of an *Englischer*. *Vell*, that's what we started talking about that evening.

"It wasn't your usual swimming was it?" asked Malcolm. His

questions brought me out of my thoughts.

"Ah, maybe not."

"It was because I was along."

I didn't say anything.

"But how else was it different?" he asked me some more.

"We wore shorts."

"You usually go in the buff."

"Some do."

"*Barmlich*," he said. It sounded funny coming from him because I'm sure he didn't know what it meant. Come to think of it, I didn't either. "They didn't do it because of me."

"They don't know you yet," I said. Really, when I thought of it, you don't take your clothes off in front of a stranger.

"What did they want to know about me?" he asked. I know he wondered about all the *Deitsch*.

"They wanted to know where you're from and all."

"Yes, but it didn't take that long to talk about where I'm from."

"*Ja*," I paused listening to the fly buzzing by the window. "They wanted to know if you have a girlfriend."

"What did you say?"

"I didn't know."

"No, I don't have one, not now, and I wish sometimes I never would have had one." He stopped for a while and then started up again. "Do they think I might be here to look for a woman?"

"Don't know."

"Oh my, I hope not." He rolled over and threw back the covers. "You have a woman, don't you?"

"*Ja*, but I don't talk about it."

"Neither do I."

I grunted.

"It's sometimes confusing," he said.

"Huh?"

"Women are confusing. How do you live with them? It's the same with all people. Relationships change, and it becomes confusing."

"Confusing?"

Malcolm propped his head on his hand and looked out the window. Several minutes passed before he spoke, and then he let it roll. "I was never that interested in women, I think, but then this Kate comes along and she seemed to be everything. Her real name was Catherine. We got along. We went to shows, read the same books, and then we'd talk about them. She didn't like television and neither did I.

"She was sensitive; I thought she was an artist. She painted too; clowns, posts, children, some just color and lines with nothing else on them. And she liked nature. We would take long walks in parks and she knew the birds and the trees. Not the way I did; I knew the names, but she really saw them, as though she communed with them. In any case, that's what I thought. But it couldn't last."

"Huh?" I grunted some more. Poor man, he'd lost his woman and had his brain off in the wild blue yonder, but he kept on talking.

"She went to another school in California about a year ago, and that ended it all."

"Didn't you see her again?"

"Yes, she came back about six months after she left, but it had all changed. It was confusing. Really, she was much the same in her interests, but the feelings we had were gone. We couldn't pick up where we had left off. She left for school again, and I haven't heard from her since then."

"Never."

"No."

"*Vell,* I'm sorry, " I said. Judas, the poor guy had a broken heart. I didn't know what else to say, but I had lost all my tiredness. My eyes were wide open, and I looked around the room. The moon came in the window bringing a light so that we could see shadows of the bedposts on the walls.

"How do you go about asking out a woman?" asked Malcolm.

"Ach, it's not hard."

"But I mean, do you knock on the door and tell the father, 'Hey, I'm coming up to see your daughter for the night'?"

I laughed, "Naw, see it makes a difference if you're going for regular or for just so. If it's for just so, then you have to take someone along and he can set up the date for you. That friend is kind of a go-between who gets things ready for you. So he just goes up and asks if she will have you."

"So you and Anna don't have to go through that every Saturday evening."

"Naw, because we're going for regular. I just take the flashlight and *blitz* in her window, and she comes down and opens the door."

"Then you stay all night."

"*Vell,* till around four or five."

"What's Anna like?"

"She's a good woman." Not that it was any of his business, but he wanted to talk, and so did I.

"Why is she a good woman?"

He had more questions than the Yoder nephews. "*Vell*, I'd have to think about that for a while," I said, but then I continued. "On the one hand, she does what is right and is good to her family and the church. On the other hand, she's a little wild; she likes to go to the music shows down in Wheeling. That wouldn't be anything to you maybe, uh? But that's the way she is."

"Sounds all right to me," he said.

"*Ja*, one night we were walking home from a singing at Gravey Ben's, and it began to rain. I said, 'Let's run!' see, to get under a tree or to a building. But she liked it. She took off her scarf and with her bare face and head looked up into the rain. It was warm and summer, of course, so I took off my hat too and just let the rain hit my face.

"But it was something, seeing that rain on her face. It was a soft rain and the streams of water would fall from her hair and slide down her skin. Our clothes were soaked and clung to us in funny shapes. Anyway, it must have rained like that for a half an hour and we just slowly walked along, and I would have missed it if she wouldn't have stayed in it."

Judas, now I was off in the wild blue yonder. I looked over at Malcolm. "You probably don't think that's something."

"Yes I do," he said.

"*Ja*, I shouldn't be telling you about it."

I was quiet for a while, thinking. "But how do you people do it?" I asked. "I mean, how do you set things up with a woman?"

"We generally call on the phone or else say something personally about going somewhere: to a show, a dance, a concert, a walk in the park. It depends some on who you are and how much money you want to spend."

"*Barmlich*, that must be quite a life," I said.

"I'm tired of it . . ."

I couldn't believe it and broke right in, "Really, you are?"

"It becomes superficial. You're always running after something to be entertained or to meet a new person. And you're constantly trying to buy pleasure." He went on like this for a while; somehow he always got "superficial" in there some place. "Yes, it gets tedious and boring."

"That's not what my brother Roy tells me."

"Maybe it's not boring for him."

"Huh."

A cloud covered the moon and the room became dark. I whispered, "Say, Malcolm, did you ever go to the burly?"

"You mean burlesque shows?"

"*Ja.*"

"Several times."

"What was it like?"

"I got bored; they're not very imaginative on how to undress. When you've seen one, the rest are all repeats. You'd have to be sick to want to see the same thing over and over again."

"What?" I asked.

"Sick. It's the same thing every time. I guess burlesque used to be much more of an art and acting and jokes, but this was only for sick people. I guess it was funny for the first time. You should go sometime, then you'd know."

"How much do they pay those girls?" I asked.

"I don't know."

"Wouldn't they ever want to marry and have a family?"

"I never thought about that," he said.

"Do their fathers and mothers know about their work?"

"Some probably do."

It was quiet again, but, Judas, my bad mind was full of whores and naked women. Wasn't right, I know, but that's what I thought. I pushed my big toes against the mattress to make sure I was still there. My toe seemed so big and important. I was now wide awake and lying flat on my back, rubbing my hands together. But I pretended and even imagined that I was almost asleep. I yawned.

"Malcolm, sleeping?"

"I can't."

I laughed, like a monkey, I laughed. He was having the same trouble I had. Then it was quiet for a while.

I asked, "Did you ever help in college, in a panty raid?"

"No, I never got into one," he laughed. "I think they did more of that several years ago at the state universities."

"Judas, can you imagine running into the buildings and pulling off all the undies. *Barmlich,* I mean, how would you look at each other the next day?"

"Golly, but you're funny. How do you think of all these things?" He said it while he laughed and we both knew this was going to nothing good. I didn't know what he was thinking, but I was totally depraved and sinful. Judas, I was seeing naked women running in college buildings and dashing out in the lawns with the breasts flying in the breeze. I knew that sometime I'd have to pay for all these bad thoughts, and that I was heading straight for the nut-house in Massilon.

Malcolm was going crazy too because he couldn't stop laughing. "Do you want to know how many goldfish I've swallowed?" he laughed.

"Never thought about that. Do you do that too?"

"No, I haven't, but several years ago they were doing that."

"*Vell*, it's just the two of us," I said, yawning and imagining we were almost asleep and trying to think how we got into this kind of talking.

"Yes, thank God."

Then it was quiet for a long time again.

"Wayne," he said in a low voice.

"Huh?"

"Do you take everything off, you know, everything, when you visit a woman on Saturday nights?"

I giggled, "Naw, is that what you people think? At first you just take off your shirt—sometimes not even that."

"*Ya* sure, but now do you take more off now?"

I laughed softly thinking how dumb he was, and how his mind was also depraved and heading straight for hell and the nuthouse. What a picture! You come to the front door, go upstairs, take all your clothes off and go to bed. That is what he thinks, eh? I could hear him laughing too.

"Oh, sometimes the *Buwe* take their clothes off, sometimes not. Look, let me explain something to you. We do it different ways. Some Amish don't go to bed at all. They date by sitting up all evening. They sit in the living room and visit the way you and I are doing right now. Others have bed courtship, but that doesn't mean that they do it. You can visit in bed just the way you and I are doing here. Some do it and some don't. I know some people think just because we date differently from other people we don't believe in being virgins. But that's the teaching of the Bible and that's what we believe. Not everyone can live up to it, but most do. You're supposed to be a virgin."

Vell, I probably said too much, but then it was quiet again.

Then after a while he started up again. "*Ya*, I was just thinking. I couldn't go along this weekend, could I?"

"Where?"

"Oh, to town, to see where you fellows go."

"What would you do?" I asked.

"Oh, I don't know . . . No, forget it. It wouldn't work."

We were quiet again for a long time and then a little screech owl gave a long wail, a sad whinny like a little horse. Then my little winged horse showed up. I saw a little four-legged horse whinnying at the top of the barn. The horse ran across the large beams at the top of the barn, and pigeons that sat along the timbers flew off when he came by. He was a little Percheron with his neck arched and the nostrils flared open and wings on the side. He looked like the horses you saw in the Greek statues in the history books. He didn't do anything or say anything to me, but he was just a strong little horse that could fly any place with his wings and trotted like a dandy. I used to see that little horse when I was a little boy whenever the screech owl called, and he always came back, even on this night when I was sure I was going crazier than a loon in heat.

The sound came again. "Hear that?" I whispered.

"Yes."

"It's a screech owl, a little owl. And there's a little winged horse running around up in the barn, high up in the timbers."

"Is that right."

That's all he said, and we both laughed softly. I don't know how to explain it, but my mind was both the clearest and the nuttiest all in the same evening.

Malcolm whispered softly again, "Wayne, sleeping?"

"Naw." Good night, I wasn't even near.

"Are . . . are you a virgin?"

"What?"

"You said you're supposed to be a virgin. Are you?"

"*Ja*, sure, but that's a pretty personal question," I said softly. "Are you?"

"I guess not." Malcolm laughed. "Maybe, but I'm not sure."

I laughed aloud now. *Barmlich*, I thought, what does he mean? Either he is or he isn't. He was laughing too. *Dummar ding*. Either he is or he isn't. Or is he a pervert who does it in all kinds of ways.

"Not sure, eh?" I laughed.

"Nope, it's a little hard to tell." He kept on laughing, and I knew for sure it was the Massilon nuthouse here we come. I stretched out my arms and legs to their fullest. My body seemed like you could see right through it, as if my bones just floated around in clear water.

Then we were quiet. Only the little screech owl kept on whinnying, and my little winged stud kept on running around the barn beams. Ah, whinny my little winged horse owl. Sometime I'll have real horses of my own that can pull like they had wings. I have a girlfriend and she has wings too, but she'll be a good wife, and now I have this loony *Englischer* on my hands.

We both stopped talking then, but I couldn't sleep right away. I didn't think he slept either, but we said not a word. I'd heard him breathe deeply, and I was happy as a lark. I didn't even know why because what we'd talked about wasn't all good and some of it was bad. I finally went to sleep with the little winged horses running and flying around in my head.

7.

The next Sunday church was held at the Milo Hershbergers. I came home from Anna's early in the morning and by five-thirty the little clock was ringing. We chored and on the way in to the house Malcolm asked me. "Are you feeling awake?"

"*Ja*, why?"

"Well, you just got in a few hours ago."

"*Ja vell*, I'm rested. Feeling okay," I said.

"I'm somewhat nervous."

"*Ja*, why?"

"What should I wear today? I don't have any dress clothes along."

"Don't worry," I said. "You can wear one of my white shirts, and just wear one of your dark pairs of pants. Just so they're clean."

We washed and sat down at the table and *die Memm* served us some coffee soup and Swiss cheese. I could tell he was pretty nervous.

"I'll try not to embarrass you."

"Naw," I tried to make him feel better. "Don't worry about us. You just try to obey God."

"You probably don't often have visitors in church."

"Naw, not often. Several years ago some Mennonites from *Pennsylvany* came to church. Never been to an Amish church before.

Chris brought them — writers and editors, kinda curious and nosey people. He's pretty good at dealing with people like that."

"What do you do on the in-between Sunday?"

"It's good for visiting and resting," I said. "In the summer all the *Buwe* get together for a ball game or to go swimming."

"What do you call this?" Malcolm pointed at his dish.

"Coffee soup."

"Yes, I should have thought." Malcolm picked up his spoon and faced the crackers and coffee in the bowl with brown sugar and cream. I think the look on his face said he wished there wouldn't be anything like a Sunday morning breakfast. But he ate it, and like a reward he got a good look at my sister.

Leona came out into the kitchen in a dark wine-colored dress which was covered by a white transparent apron and cape. She looked spiffy and inside the cape was a little pink ribbon that came down over her breasts. She winked at me as if to make sure she was still my sister even if she was good-looking. The way Malcolm looked at her I could tell that he also thought my sister was pretty snazzy, even if neither of us said anything. Some of these things it's just as good not to say much about them.

By the time we finished breakfast the two teams were hitched to the rail in front of the house, and we were ready for church. Ben had the road horse in the surrey, and he, *die Memm*, Benny and Leona went with the surrey. Malcolm, John and I got into the buggy and Flecha was ready to fly.

We headed south to the Hershbergers with Flecha trotting briskly on that cool morning, and you'd never have thought that only about four hours ago she had come home on the same road. As we got near the Hershbergers, we saw other buggies also coming to the church meeting. And some neighbors were walking. The regular sounds of the horses clopping on the pike gave a nice life to the early morning, and we didn't talk. We were all in the world of our minds, and our ears heard the music of the clip-clopping of the horses' hoofs.

At the Hershberger's driveway, Flecha put her head sideways and turned in on the hard ground. One of Mike's boys came to help unhitch her, and I led her into the barnyard where two flat-bed wagons were standing. I stayed with Flecha to tie her because I was particular about her not getting kicked. Some horses are kickers and I didn't want Flecha near them. I tied her at the end beside Bess, Chris Yoder's plug.

When I got back to the front of the barn, my three nephews had already found Malcolm. They were standing with Chris, probably pumping Malcolm with all kinds of questions or else telling him about their projects of hoopies and pets. Malcolm looked stiff as a board with the plain white shirt I had given to him to wear and the store-bought pants.

But when I walked over to them my little fishermen and project directors did not have much to say, and I think we all felt everyone was watching us. Benny came to the rescue by coming up and announcing, "*Schtadt geh,*" and shaking hands until everything seemed natural.

"So you brought him along," Aden said to me.

"*Ja,* sure, why not."

"*Ja,* he'll learn a lot," Aden said and then turned to Malcolm.

"Have you ever been to our church before?"

"No, I never have. Why? Should I be especially aware of something?"

"Oh no. You do whatever you like."

"But I want to do whatever you do."

"Well, then do whatever we do."

"Will you sit beside your father this morning?" Malcolm asked.

"*Ja,* we still do . . ."

Malcolm then looked at me, "Where do you think I should sit?" I could tell that he didn't think he would be welcome with the *Buwe.*

"Either way," I said. "You can sit with the *Buwe* and me or you can sit with Chris and the boys."

"*Ja,* you just sit with us," said Chris. He liked to take new people under his wing, and I knew that things would go just as well with the *Buwe* if he kept a distance for a while.

So it was decided, and I was glad I didn't have to try to get him close to the *Buwe* who were standing over by the shed looking spiffy as could be. The *Buwe* spit into the dust, rubbed their shoes in it until it disappeared, and soon they spit again.

They didn't say anything about Malcolm that morning, and I knew they didn't think much of his living with us and all. But then, by crappy, they didn't even know him, and he was our visitor. We could be good to him for that at least. Still I could feel that a little something was wrong.

I stayed with Chris for a while, and we went over to another group of men at the bottom of the bank by the milkhouse. It was kind of a gathering place where we got ready to go up in the barn. We sidled up to Bush Mike's Mart, the *braucher,* but he paid no attention to us whatsoever. I knew the little boys were interested in him even if Malcolm didn't know him from Sam Hill. The men were talking about threshing and how the wheat was about ready.

Halfway up the barn hill the ministers were standing in a small group looking down at the ground and occasionally looking out at the people. Probably checking us over to see if we were all in the *Attnung*. Better check that *Englischer* over there by Chris, but I knew that he was the least of their worries.

"Who will preach this morning?" asked Malcolm trying to make a little conversation with the boys.

"Can't tell," said Raymond. He tried to keep a straight face while the others looked down so he wouldn't see them smiling. "It could be one minister; it may be another."

I looked toward the front of the house. There were groups of women, Martha and little Samuel and other mothers with their little children, some old grannies, and then the *Meed*, the young women, looking all spiffed up there on the front porch.

Off to the one side of the house in the yard was a tripod with a huge iron kettle hanging from it and fresh kindling under the kettle. Milo was scurrying around like a pack rat, getting things around for his bean soup. *Ja*, that should keep you busy this forenoon Milo, I thought. Most of our houses had summer kitchens or washhouses with brick ovens where we made the bean soup in a big kettle, but Milo Hershberger still hung his outside like some pioneer. He was downright proud of his bean soup and the way he made it, even if the women usually did it nowadays. I always thought he wanted to do it himself because that way he didn't have to go to the church meeting. But anyway, I'll have to admit he made good bean soup and everyone else said so too.

Then it was time to go in. The ministers first walked in. Next a group of the old women went, followed by a group of old men, including my dad with Benny trailing along behind. He looked back at us, and we knew that he would have liked to stay with us. Then the middle-aged men went in and this included Chris and the little boys and Malcolm.

The *Meed* came down from the porch and walked right past us in front of the shed. They stepped along like the handsome spring heifers they were. Some big Holsteins like Leona, a few little Jerseys like Sarah, and some nervous Ayrshires. I knew they really weren't like cows, and Leona was smarter than I was anyway, but it was kind of an auction the way they walked past. They didn't look over at us, but I knew they were thinking of us as they moved by. One of the *Buwe* made a soft whistling sound and a few did too much coughing; you'd a thought we were all coming down with the whooping cough.

They filed in behind the older women and sat down. There was not enough room for the last one—poor Pitty Hostetler's Mary. She got all redder than a beet, stood there for a few seconds, and then headed for a bench closer to the front where there was a space beside an old woman. The *Buwe* giggled and punched each other in the ribs when they saw it. Poor girl, I pitied her because we all thought she was kind of a nitwit anyway.

Then it was all quiet and no one moved, but we knew it was time we'd have to go. No one told us but we knew we had to. We went up the hill in a single file and crowded in a long row of benches behind the older men and some of the fathers and their children. I ended up sitting right smack behind Malcolm and Chris and the boys. After being all spread out outside we were packed in the barn like sardines. The women and girls sat on the other side of us and when I looked up I could see them right there in front.

I looked over across the group, but everyone looked down at the floor and then just quickly slipped a look at each other. Even Malcolm looked down, but he did kind of stand out with his red hair and his not having a hat to wear. I thought then that we should have given him one.

The *Meed*, the young women, looked even better in here than they did outside with their clean white transparent capes standing out against the dark dresses, and their faces looked healthy and fresh as fruit. The rich clean hay in the mow gave a nice smell, and I knew everyone had taken a bath on Saturday night. Even the old men and women seemed to get younger as they blended in with the youth of the group. I reached down and picked up some timothy hay and pinched it and started chewing on the stem.

All was quiet.

Then there was a whinny, a snort and the crack of a kick, and one of the helpers shouted down in the barn. I hoped it wasn't Flecha who was getting kicked. Then all of us reached up and in one motion took our hats off. We put them under the benches or stacked them on top of each other.

Then all was quiet again.

Repat started passing out the song books. He was our oldest member and the main *vorsinger*, and what with our visitor and everything, I knew he'd take the first tune. "Number seven in the thick book," he called. "Number seven in the thick book and 135 in the little one." We picked up the books and found the number.

Repat's lone tenor voice led out in the quietness; he did a few little trills and then the rest of us men joined in on the second word. We picked up some speed as we got to the end of the first line and then on the last word we dropped everything. There was a break and then Repat's lone wren voice led out again. This time the women joined us on the second line with their high voices, and we were all together in making praise to God.

Two great things unite us: our work and our music, and I think the greatest of these is the music. I thought of it some time later when I went to another church and found out how different they sing. The lone *vorsinger's* voice was set off against the heavy thickness of the rest of the men's voices and then the women came in with their high tones and we'd throw the sound back and forth to each other as it went up to God.

Malcolm later told me that it was one of the strangest and the nicest things he'd ever heard in his life. He claimed we still carried it from the monks of the Middle Ages. I don't know about that, and it's just a theory anyway, he said. All I know is that it's the sound of our unity, with everyone coming together led by the trills of the *vorsinger*, and that Repat can fly up and down like a wren in the spring.

I sang loudly blending in with the thick sound of the men. I looked across at my sister Martha who was looking down at the book and singing the high part with the women. I thought of faith and hope and God, and for a moment I forgot all about Anna and hawks and Flecha and threshing. That was the good part of this singing because it purified your thinking in forgetting all the things you had to do or your worries and took you into another place where all was one with God. I'm not sure that I can explain it, and I never thought about it much until Malcolm asked me so many questions about it later.

The words and the tune took us back to the martyrs who gave their lives for the Christian faith. That number seven was supposed to be written by the Anabaptist Michael Sattler, and Chris later made a copy of it in German and English for Malcolm when he asked so much about it.

Als Christus mit Sein'r Wahren Lehr

1. *Als Christus mit sein'r wahren Lehr*
   Versammlet hatt' ein kleines Heer,
   Sagt er das jeder mit Geduld
   Ihm täglich's Kreutz nach tragen sollt.

2. *Un sprach: Ihr Liebe Jünger mein,*
Ihr solet allzeit munter seyn,
Auf Erden auch nichts lieben mehr,
Denn mich und folgen meiner Lehr.

3. *Die Welt die wird euch stellen nach,*
Und anthun manchen Spott und Schmach,
Verjagen und ach sagen frey,
Wie dass der Satan in euch sey.

4. *Wenn man euch non lästert und schmacht,*
Meinethalben verfolgt und schlaegt,
Seyd froh, denn siehe euer Lohn
Ist euch bereit ins Himmels Thron.

When Christ with His Teaching True

1. When Christ with his teaching true
Gathered his flock his will to do,
Each one have patience, thus said he,
Take up your cross and follow me.

2. Beloved disciples who are mine
Take courage as your lives do shine;
Oh, love the world far less than me
And heed my teachings true, said he.

3. The world will lie in wait for you,
Will mock you lambs and scorn you too,
Outlaw you from the land expell
As though you were a force of hell.

4. But if ill-treated for my sake
And daily you to shame awake,
Be joyful, your reward is nigh
Prepared for you in heaven on high.

That's just a sample because the song goes on for 13 verses, but we usually didn't sing all the verses anyway. The singing was slow, and Chris once told me he timed a hymn that lasted for a half hour. And some said that the *Ausbund* was too old and too much about martyrs and I don't know what, but it was our music. I knew that some would have liked to speed them up, and Malcolm told me later that we did everything just opposite from the way other people sang. He liked it that way.

Most people held out the last note of a line, and we just dropped it. On the other hand, we held the first note as if it were something precious. Chris liked harmony the way we sang in parts at the singings, and in church we only all sang together. Chris even once tried to sing tenor or something to the *"Lob Lied"* and that came to nothing. Judas, Repat came to him later and told him in no uncertain terms that singing like that is proud, and if he wanted to sing like that he can go join the Mennonites or some high church. Repat didn't call on Chris to take the lead for about a year just to make sure his point was clear.

The *"Lob Lied"* was the second hymn we sang at every church meeting, and I could have sung it backwards in my sleep. It was also a good song for the younger ones to get a chance at leading, and Repat winked at young Simon down the bench from me to take the lead. His young quivering and unsteady voice led out:

> *O Gott Vater, wir loben dich*
> *Und deine Güte preisen . . .*
>
> Our father God, thy name we praise,
> To thee our hymns addressing . . .

While we sang the next hymn the ministers came back and soon we stopped. Joseph Yoder, our oldest preacher, was in front and the old owl sat down on the bench like there was something heavy on his shoulders. When it was time for the *Aanfang,* Joseph Yoder took a deep breath, slowly got up and walked to the front of the open barn doors in the middle of the men and women.

In humility his sagging face turned down to the floor, his eyelids drooped, and I could see the hat ring mark in the back of his long black hair. His soft black eyes, a little watery, looked up, and then he looked down again and rubbed his hands together and spoke: "The Lord is great and greatly to be praised; we could say with the Psalmist."

He coughed a little, looked up into the rafters, and a pigeon flew across the mow and then some more words came out: "Yes, as we are again gathered in this warm, but we could say pleasant day, we can see so many things that the Lord has given us. Bless the Lord, oh my soul and all that is within me. Bless the Lord oh my soul and forget not all his benefits."

It was a nice beginning and then another pause. Boy, was Joseph slow. Then he said that God had chosen to speak to us through a weak vessel, one who had much to learn yet. He didn't say it like it was an excuse for being a slow old owl, but just the way you'd say it was going to rain if it's cloudy and you hear the thunder.

"And as we are here gathered, we are reminded again of the words which God spoke to Adam and Eve when he placed them into the garden. On days like today, when the land is green and our crops are growing, one can almost see the beauty of that garden. Not that we really know, and it was most certainly more beautiful than anything we know of, yet sometimes when I walk through a cornfield I think this may be like Eden, something like the garden."

He stopped for a minute as if it was a new thought he'd just gotten of the Garden of Eden as a Holmes County cornfield. Then he went on: "*Ja*, in this place, God placed Adam and Eve and said . . ."

I looked down at the hay strewn floor and listened as Joseph began with Adam and Eve in the garden, went to Cain and Abel and later to Abraham and Sarah and Isaac and David and Jonathan. Later he'd talk about Ruth and then he'd come to Jesus Christ. He told how that people were wicked but that God was merciful and forgave. He often said that God gave rules and commandments for our benefit like the Ten Commandments and he wanted us, especially the young people, not to miss that point.

Joseph's *Aanfang* went on in a kind of singsong rhythm, and I knew that if he began with Adam and Eve, about an hour later he'd finish up with Jesus Christ. We could listen to the words or we could listen to it like music where it went right through you. We didn't listen that closely because we knew that Joseph didn't have anything that new to tell us on how to live differently or what to do tomorrow; it was more that he had the Bible story to tell and we should listen to it because it was from God and good.

Still, I often listened because he was a smart old owl and always brought out something about history or something that had happened. After talking about how God had taken care of Abraham and his journey, he all at once said, "I've been thinking about why Columbus discovered America. Here was this land of the Indians and the buffalo and wolf, and all at once the Europeans find it." He stopped for a moment and Bush Mike's Mart blinked his eyes and looked up.

"*Ja*, I believe it was because God knew that there were suffering Anabaptists who were persecuted and killed in Europe and needed a place to live where they could worship and live in peace. *Ja*, we should always give thanks to God for taking care of his people. We just have to be faithful." I knew that Malcolm was trying to understand the words, and he picked up more of the high German than our usual Pennsylvania *Deitsch*. He wondered afterwards why the Indians had to be killed just because the Anabaptists had suffered so I told him the Hostetler story, even if I couldn't give him satisfaction on everything.

The sermon was long, and I looked around at the other people. Bush Mike's Mart's eyes were closed again, and he was resting. Martha was looking down at the hay strewn floor with little Samuel sleeping in her lap. I knew that she wished that she had a little baby girl sleeping in her lap too. Maybe God would give her one, but for now all she had was a little sleeper and those three sons who were wiggling all over the bench.

Joseph said that he would need to finish soon so that he would not take too much time from the brother: "Then if we are united, let us pray." We all fell to our knees in silent prayer.

After the prayer one of the deacons read a scripture and then some of us left for a break. First, several married men with little children went out; next, the three young Yoders marched out; then a row of young girls left; and finally our whole row of *Buwe* got up and filed out. We drank water and peed and got our blood circulation running, and when we got back in Gravey Ben was already halfway in his main sermon.

Gravey Ben was our young 35-year old bishop. He stood strong in the middle of the floor. His bright blue eyes flashed about, and he seemed to have to force them to humbly look down at the hay strewn floor at times. He was still learning to preach, was 20 years too young to be bishop and spoke with short jerky sentences at the beginning.

Before long, though, he also got in a singsong tune, even if his short sharp notes were not like Joseph's long drawn out tones. Gravey told us how terrible it was when we did not follow God and the *Attnung*. There are terrible things that can happen to us if we do not follow God. "Sodom and Gomorrah are the results if we sin and allow ourselves to follow our lust." He got all excited when he told the Bible stories and the good and bad that happened.

My mind drifted to last night when I had been with Anna. She wanted to go to the Wheeling music show. Her brown eyes were bright when she said it. I saw the strand of hair that had gone across her face; oh, she was sly. But she was a good woman and would be a good wife. How could she be so wild and so good at the same time? I'll never know.

I tried to look at Gravey, but the picture of the little sharp talking minister turned into a young woman who was winking at me. My head nodded forward. I felt numb, and my head jerked forward and backward.

That woke me, and I saw the little Yoder boys cut out little pieces of hay and make pliers, and other little shapes and squares with the hay. I looked at Chris and he was listening to Gravey, but he looked sleepy too.

I could see Ben was staring at the rafters with his arms folded tightly in front of him. Benny was chewing on a cookie. Ben's sharp eyes were clear and blinked hard. Was he listening or was he seeing a field of wheat shocks set up in nice rows which would be ready to thresh tomorrow or Tuesday? I could see them myself with the heads full of grain and dry and light and ready for the harvesting. This week the threshers would come to our place if the weather held.

The bowl of saltines, grahams and white church cookies now came by us and the little Yoder boys each helped themselves. I felt sleepy again, and my body slumped and the eyelids closed.

A banty hen woke me up. She came out of her nest above the granary and started to cackle. Judas, was she mad as she scolded all of us for coming so near to her nest. Gravey didn't pay any attention to her but went right on with the sermon, even if all of us were now listening only to the banty. *Ja* cackle, henny penny. You won't disturb Gravey. I watched her jerk her head as she screamed at us and then my eyes closed again and I listened.

Nice music. She carried on in those wild notes over Gravey Ben's stories for a while longer, and then all at once there was a whirring sound. It sounded like a rubber band propeller airplane when all at once she flew out over the threshing floor and sailed over Gravey. She missed his head by about two feet and landed on the straw stack out in the barnyard.

There she cackled some more but we didn't pay any attention to her for very long. Gravey didn't either. He didn't even flinch or break beats in his story when she zoomed past his head. He just kept on telling the story of the birth of Christ in the humble manger, as if nothing had happened.

Chris got out a pack of Wrigley's chewing gum and gave a piece to each of his sons. The boys separated the silver from the paper of the chewing gum wrapper and made little boxes. Matthew handed one to Malcolm. Malcolm looked at his watch and I pulled mine out too. It was almost 12 and Gravey was getting close to the finish. "And so Jesus went to the house of Matthew. One might say that this was not a *litterlich* man, but he was outside the church. We, of course, don't know all the reasons of why Jesus Christ went. But he and Matthew ate together and then this man saw the error of his ways.

"One might say that he repented. He gave back to those from whom he had cheated. It sometimes comes to me that we forget that when we are with our Lord Jesus Christ, then we will not live like the tax collectors but like the disciples. One is reminded of King David as we already heard from our brother . . ."

Finally Gravey sat down and then it was time for the testimonies to the sermon. One deacon from another district especially put his hands up on his face and thought deeply on what he was going to say. We had some more prayers and announcements. The preachers wanted to make sure we knew about the new 1-W forms and where church would be held in two weeks. The deacon was going to come around for more help to a family in another district that had a large hospital bill. We sang a last hymn, and I could smell Milo Hershberger's soup.

I took Malcolm and we headed with the *Buwe* for the basement where we were the second group to be served. When the first group finished, the girls scurried in to change the soup spoons and replace them with clean ones for our group. They also changed the bowls with steaming hot soup. I told Malcolm just to help himself the way the rest of us do, but I didn't think it would turn out quite like that.

When we moved in to the table, Simon—he's one of Mony Hershberger's 13 — dove right in to the soup with the table manners of a hog. He took a big spoonful of soup right in his mouth, and it must have been really hot because blurp, he shot it right back into the bowl. Simon turned red, and I felt bad that he was such a pig.

Everybody just looked at each other with a big grin except Simon. Even though the soup was good, not one person ate from that bowl for the rest of our standing. We all reached way across the table to the other two bowls. Only Simon ate from the slop bowl.

Malcolm said it reminded him of eating a hot cheese and wine dish called a fondue where everyone dipped bread in the bowl, and he said he didn't mind all eating from the same bowl. But I thought he probably thought we were all hogs like Mony's Simon. Milo Hershberger's soup was good though, along with some beets, cheese and bread, and soon it was time to make room for another group that was waiting.

After dinner we stood around and talked for a while. Several of the men and Ben and I joined in a circle with Aaron, and we made plans for having the threshing ring start at our place that week. By three o'clock I told Malcolm and John it was time to go home, and we left with Flecha and got started on the early chores.

8.

The threshers came to our house the next week. We were about the first family in our ring to have the wheat cut, shocked and dried so the rig was coming on Wednesday. Threshing was a big time for us. For me, it meant having the team go to other families in our ring to help. It got kind of long when you finally got the barley finished, but at the beginning of the summer I looked forward to it like a frolic. We'd get up in the morning looking forward to the hot sun and getting together with the neighbors. We'd look forward to seeing Aaron.

For *die Memm* and Leona it was getting big meals ready and being ready to keep them hot if we had to work late in the evening. Sometimes in the afternoons we'd decide to finish at a place or it looked like rain, and we'd keep right on going till dark. They prepared the drink and refreshments for us in the field.

For Ben the threshing was planning and directing. Boy, would he start churning. We could feel it coming several days before the thresher day like the heavy air before a storm. It was work too. He had to let everyone know when the wheat was ready, get the granaries clean, get set for the straw. And it was money. We fed most of our oats and barley, but I think Dad's extra churning on the wheat was that he knew when it was finished, we'd take it to the elevator. There'd be some golden butter in our pockets.

For my little nephews, the Yoder boys, the threshing was a time to see Bush Mike's Mart. Mart was kind of secret, and you could tell they were just waiting to ask him questions or get a good look. They also wanted to be a hired hand, especially Aden. He was getting about big enough.

On Tuesday evening Aaron came with the rig. He was perched on top of the International Harvester like some eagle, and the way he looked so big, bouncing on top of the tractor, I guess we were just mice. He came up the lane and stopped at the bottom of the barn hill. We all came out and closed in on the rig except for Malcolm. He hung back. Aaron slowly turned in his seat and looked around as if he were going to peck at one of us, and then he bent down and dammered around under the hood.

"Not getting it's gas right today," he muttered to himself. Only then did he look down at my father. You'd have thought he was 50 feet up there, the way he acted. *Vell*, it was all right; he was the thresher. When he got on top of that International he was the boss, and we knew he'd worked with that machine for many summers. It was kind of something because usually Dad would have ordered Aaron around, but not today when he was on top of the International. Now the old eagle sat up there and shot out the questions like orders.

"Do you want to thresh it in the barn?"

"Yep."

"Which granary will you fill first?"

"The one down at the end."

"Do you want all the straw on a stack or do you want some up in the barn?"

"Everything outside on a pile."

Malcolm came up beside me and he was really getting interested in all this too, but he wanted to sound kind of ho-hum.

"I suppose he's done this for many years," he said.

"You're tootin' right," I said. "He's been our thresher for as long as I can remember." Then I listened back to the men, and they got into the weather and how the crops were looking.

We helped Aaron hitch the threshing machine to the front of the tractor so that he could push the big machine right up in front of the granaries. It really looked big up in there.

The next day at one o'clock the gravel crackled in our lane as the wagons came in. The first team in was my little nephew Aden and he had Bush Mike's Mart on the back. Aden drove right up to Malcolm and me beside the barn where we were waiting to head for the field. But then Ben came out of the barn.

"Who sent you?"

"Dad."

"Where's he?"

"At home."

"Doing what?"

"Working."

"Reading?"

"Making hay." For a 12-year-old he was doing really good. "*Ja,* today should be a good day to get in some more of the alfalfa."

"Huh," Ben grunted.

I knew that my nephew admired his grandfather, but he defended his father. He spit on the ground and rubbed his shoe nervously in the wet dust, trying to seem old.

"So you think you can be a hand?"

"That's why Dad sent me, Grandpa."

I jumped in then: "Come on, Aden, you'll go with me." Dad had said enough and the sun wasn't getting any cooler. I jumped on the wagon with him. And Ben looked away.

"John! Get that dog out of the sow pen. What in the Sam River do you think we want? Some little half-dogs running around here."

Next, he spotted Leona on the porch and she looked all befuddled. "What kind of pop should you serve? Judas River, do you think I want to run the kitchen too?"

John threw some stones at Bounce who was in the pen where the sow was in heat, and Leona turned away all red in the face. I winked at Aden. He was trying to keep a straight face.

"Dirty hound!" Ben shouted as Bounce ran behind the barn with his tail between his legs. "John, next go up to the barn and get a wood block to send with the wagon."

He looked at Aaron, "Now, if the sun stays out." Then he shouted at the house where Leona had disappeared. "Root beer! Leona. Root beer! Don't we always drink root beer!"

He jerked his arm in front of himself all the time and the third wagon came up the lane. He looked over at Aaron again and the old eagle blinked one big eye.

That was all Dad needed. "The shocks are dry and the machine is ready. *Vell,* let's not stand around until it rains." That was all we needed. The three teams headed for the field.

I joined young Aden, Bush Mike's Mart and one of Mony Hershberger's boys, Eli. We loaded the wagons with two pitchers who threw up the sheaves and two loaders who were usually the greenhorns.

"*Vell*, Aden, we'll see if you can load straight," I called up to him as I threw up the sheaves.

"You know what we do with loaders who can't keep a load straight, don't you?" asked Eli. "Sure, we make them go without ice cream or pop."

That started Mart off on his favorite subject. "We are getting that pop this afternoon, aren't we?" asked Mart.

I just acted as if I didn't hear and threw my fork into the next sheaf. "Nothing like some good root beer—Hires."

The Hershberger boy was laughing.

"Next best thing to root beer is orange."

"It's better to talk of refreshments after we've worked," I said. You can't let this kind of baloney go on too long. Mart always wanted pop or store drink when he helped others thresh, but then when we went over to his place, what do we get? Just plain old lemonade or Koolaid.

"*Ja*, Mart, how about throwing me a sheaf?" said Eli still laughing.

"Nothing like good cold root beer," Mart said, smacking his lips together and digging into the first shock.

I looked up at my little nephew and he was smiling at me. He knew what we were working with. He also knew that this was about the only thing he could get Mart to talk about. Mart was a *braucher* and a secret old clump about the main part of his life.

"Maybe that store root beer is better for your health," Aden said to me. "Just what the doctor ordered."

I didn't say anything to him even if I wanted to laugh. No use in feeding that little boy's critical ideas. He got enough of that from Chris. Chris always called the *braucher* Doctor Mart, but it was more to make fun of him than anything else.

There was no point in being too hard on a person when he helped people, even the *Englische* know that. We'd often see big cars like Buicks and Cadillacs driving into Mart's lane on Saturdays and in the evenings. *Die Memm* would go to him with her rheumatism and bad back, and she claimed that it always helped her. Even Dad took Benny several times for his mind, but Mart couldn't do much about him. Benny was just born that way.

But I knew what Aden was thinking because I'd heard enough from Chris. He claimed that Mart's *brauching* was the kind of black magic that you can find in some of the old books of Moses. He said it was of the devil, and he didn't want his family to have anything to do with it. Martha would get after the little boys that if they didn't stop peeing in bed she'd take them to see Mart.

Anyway the *braucher* was kind of a secret, and I could see why the boys were interested in him. His short fat body moved from one shock to another, and in that little head and high pitched voice he must have known a lot about the power that it takes to get better. But Aden was working now, and Mart and I were pitching.

There was a swing to work like this, and soon we got going as a team so that we really worked together. I began each shock with the umbrella sheaf on top and gave it a smooth toss to the top of the wagon. It landed nicely beside Aden with the grain end going first. That way if it touched him it didn't scratch him. Then I turned to the side sheaves and one by one sent them flying up to Aden.

I liked this pitching. The experienced or older men always got to do it. An inexperienced hand or a dummy would often hit the loader, but if you knew what you were doing, you would just pitch them so that they landed with a soft plop right beside your loader, or sometimes even in the place where he wanted it on the side of the load. I always threw them one at a time, even if some pitchers would pick up two sheaves.

A grey field mouse, with white nose and paws, ran out when I picked up the last sheaf of the shock. It ran like blind in one direction then another. Finally, it went squeaking down a little hole.

I looked up at Aden as he stomped down a sheaf and put another one in its place. He was working like a man, and I was tossing them up at about the regular speed. And he was keeping up with the Hershberger boy and Mart. Sweat was dripping from the edge of his nose, and he blew it out into the humid air. Eli moved the team ahead to the next shock and Aden fell down. Careless dummy, that Hershberger, but Aden got right back up and was ready for the next sheaf.

The load was full. "That'll do it," I said. Aden came down the front uprights, and we walked behind the load and sized it up. Not bad. There were a few sheaves sticking out, but the load was straight and it would ride well. We took off our hats and let the breeze cool our hair as Eli and the wagon headed for the barn. This little nephew was a good worker.

We stood around a shock waiting for an empty wagon to come back to the field. Mart put another wad of tobacco in his mouth. He spit a nice long curl of water on the ground. Aden watched him closely, and I knew he would have liked to talk about *brauching*.

Why did we always want to do the things we couldn't? Anyway, I wanted to talk about the elections.

"*Vell*, Mart, how are you going to vote this fall?" I asked.

"I'm not voting."

"No?"

"None of our issues are up."

"*Ja*, but this is not the usual election. You see, here we'll have a Catholic running against a Protestant and some people are saying we need to take a stand on this one. This is the first election like this in our history. I think we should vote on this one."

I had given this subject some thinking. It was partly that everybody was talking about it, I guess. But it was also, I thought, one of those cases where every now and then we should become more involved in the world. "This is more than a political case; this is really a religious issue that could be pretty big."

"I don't care if it's a Catholic, a Jew or a Mexican. We don't vote for presidents," Mart snorted.

"You don't think it makes any difference if Kennedy's elected?" I asked.

Then little Aden jumped in: "We might get persecuted by the Catholics again. They're very powerful and it could happen again. Do you know that they owned half of Europe at one time, and they still have aims to rule the world? That's what LaMar Wengert says." Boy, was Aden getting excited. "Now what kind of connections do the Kennedys have with the Pope?"

I think Aden would have gone on for a while, but Mart paid no attention to him. What did this little boy know about running the world or how it runs? He was just telling us what his dad had said and Chris was just repeating what LaMar Wengert had said and LaMar was just repeating some *Englischer's* views. That's what the Mennonites will always tell you. I knew that was what Mart was thinking because he didn't give a snort about what Aden said. He turned to me.

"What difference does it make? Not much. Naw, we stay out of the national elections. If it's some issue about the schools that affect our children or something that's important, then we'll vote, but not with worldly politics. Catholics or Protestants — they all smell the same. That's not our business." Mart threw some soft wheat grains in his mouth and chewed on them with his tobacco.

"*Ja*," I said. "You have something there. I don't know that the Protestants and the Republicans are that much better, the way they took the horses from us in *Pennsylvany*. Whatever their religion, they just follow their own laws."

Mart kept right on chewing. He wasn't just from yesterday, and I kept on talking. "Maybe you're right. I don't want to have anything to do with the high government either. But, you know, I just heard LaMar say too about this is one case where we should all vote, what with Kennedy the candidate. He may be right."

"Vell, you won't see me around the town on election day," Mart said. "If we vote for one of them then we're responsible to them too. Menno Simons and all those never had anything to do with running the government and neither do we. LaMar may be a Mennonite, but he doesn't know anything about Menno Simons. Now if it's about our children, some bond levy or something like that, vell, that's different."

I didn't answer right away. Malcolm and some of the men from the other load came up. Then Aden jumped in. "I don't think we can go on like this, living off of the good of the land and not helping to run it. How do you know what affects us? If the Catholics take over the country, that'll affect us." He looked over at Mart, even if the braucher didn't give a hoot for the little boy's opinions. "Why shouldn't we be concerned with what goes on in other parts of the world? We even have a good way of being nonresistant now." He looked over at me. "There's a lot of countries, believe me, where you don't have that privilege."

"And some don't even have to go to 1-W," chimed in Gravey Ben's Simon. "Isn't that right, Wayne?"

"Ja, vell, if he can produce," said Mart. They all laughed. "It's either 1-W or 1-B. B boply."

I let'm laugh. I never did know what to say on these things, but did they have to get into my private life? My neck vein tightened and my body felt cold while the hot sun was shining. I just looked straight ahead in the field and didn't look them in the eyes. Gravey Ben's boy there, he'd a said something vulgar right back, and I wasn't going to give him a chance. I wouldn't joke about my girl or personal things like that. I left them go and kind of changed things when I said, "How about some 1-D? Drink what you want."

I pulled out the two cases of soda pop which came out with one of the wagons and gave the men their root beer, orange and grape. Aden took his bottle to Mart who took the cap off with his teeth. Mart was the only one in our ring who could do it like that. He just bit them off, and we liked to watch him, especially the young boys.

"When you get big, you'll learn to do a few things like that yourself."

Aden laughed, but I think he was learning some of the wisdom of the *braucher.*

"*Ja,* you'll learn how to open bottles and how to understand the world."

"Think so?" said Aden. He was looking Mart right in his red face, and Mart drank down two bottles of root beer and one orange.

"Anyway," I said. "We'll hear a lot more of politics this fall."

"And we'll see if we hear a lot more of wedding bells too," said that smart aleck Gravey Ben's Simon again.

"Whether you vote or not, do you really think Nixon is so much better than Kennedy? I'm assuming that Kennedy will win the nomination."

It was Malcolm and everyone listened.

"It seems to me that it isn't clear that a Catholic would be worse than this Quaker. What kind of a Quaker is he anway? Does he practice the beliefs of the Friends? Does he talk about nonviolence and peace or care for the poor and the Negroes? No, he's interested in bigger defense budgets and living off the military industrial complex." He used some other big and modern words that I might not have right, but he kept on going. "Now, tell me, on Quemoy and Matsue, is there any substantial difference in their positions? Both sound the same to me. In fact, if it's a matter of religion in how they act, I'd be inclined to think there is more to support in Kennedy."

No one said anything. I looked at my neighbors. They were all looking down or in another direction. *Ja,* he had some good points there, and he had given it some thought, and if we'd a listened he'd a found some good things to say for welfare and unions and socialism too. But we weren't going to get in a big political argument with this Quaker. Mart spit at a shock and said, "It's not getting any earlier." And we went back to work.

By nine o'clock the sun went down, and we had to stop because it was getting damp. A large straw stack sat like a big iceberg on the outside of our barn, and two of the granaries were full of wheat.

Die Memm and Leona served us a huge meal. Poor women, they had to keep it warm since six o'clock, but we all felt good and the women made little jokes of how we didn't eat enough. "What's Bounce going to do with all this food?" We were all happy and Aden sat beside me and ate like a horse. I think he even ate more than Mart.

I went out to see Aden and the rest of the men off. I untied Aden's team and held them. There stood my nephew between the two uprights with his head up and holding the reins. The moon was not bright, but I could see his dark shape just as clear as could be. Mart jumped on back of the wagon and his feet were swinging down the sides. "Let's go," he clucked.

But I held on to the team. There beside me had appeared my father. I could feel him there even before he said anything. I held on to the horses.

"Tell Chris he sent a good hand today," Ben said in an even but clear voice that you could have heard all the way to Holmesburg.

I left the horses go. The team circled around us and headed down the lane. Aden whistled softly, the gravel crackled and Mart's little legs swung from the wagon sides like a trapeze midget. The horses snorted and broke into a trot when the wagon came to the blacktop. They were followed by the other teams.

"*Schtadt gehe.* Going to town," said Benny who had come to us. "Yup, and tomorrow won't wait," said Ben as he headed toward the house. I knew he was thinking of how soon we could get finished tomorrow and then move on to Mony Hershbergers. I grabbed Benny around the neck and we headed for the house too.

9.

I went to Anna's on Saturday night. It had been a busy threshing week and I soon fell asleep, but I woke up thinking of Malcolm. He had wanted to come with me to some of the young people's gatherings, but it didn't work. That's like mixing oil and water. Maybe if he lived here longer it would work, but not now.

He didn't come to look for a young woman anyway. What would he be telling the *Buwe* if he'd show up at one of our gatherings? Furthermore, sometimes they get rough and rowdy. I know we shouldn't drink, but sometimes a few do and things get crazy.

So I had to make excuses. How would it work if I'd go along to one of your college parties? *Ja vell*, we just kind of stand around anyway, and everyone likes to talk in *deitsch*, and you wouldn't understand it anyway. Judas, I almost told him to stay home with Benny because he liked him so much. When I left he was playing with Benny and Leona and that should have kept him happy. They were pitching horseshoes when I left the house.

I heard a deep breath. Was she waking up? This woman who lies beside me and makes me feel good all over. She makes me think crazy things. She makes me want to have a good horse and work hard and join the church. How can women be so powerful? Why does she get so much of my attention? I think of her during the day, and she makes me feel wild and true all at the same time.

I felt hard and soft all at the same time as my feelings jumped up to the ceiling. I looked up at the dark color of the ceiling. There was another deep breath. She was waking. What did she think? Did she hear music? It was the music of a banjo and a guitar. Strange it was to me that I was just next to her and warm and strong. And at the same time she was nice and sly and even a little strange. She was like cold water that moves all the time and you can never put your finger on it to hold it still.

She moved but didn't open her eyes. Should I marry this woman? Everybody expected it but was that a good reason? I hoped she didn't think it had anything to do with 1-W. In the dim light I saw that her eyes were opening. *Ja,* I had all these thoughts and you were awake too.

"Anna," I whispered. "Why are we getting married?"

"Why shouldn't we?" She was all awake because she jumped right into the conversation.

"Do you think it's just because I don't want to go to 1-W?"

"I hadn't thought of it." She sounded irritated.

"*Vell,* it isn't," I said.

"Who said it was?"

"Oh, I don't know," I said. "I was just thinking it shouldn't be just that." She didn't say anything. "And maybe I should do 1-W. If we don't believe in war, this would be a sacrifice. It would be a service. Have to leave home. Help take care of the sick people. Not earn much." I don't know why I said all that, but it was the kind of thing that Chris would have said. I wasn't even sure I believed it, but I said it anyway.

She got up on her side and braced her head on her arm. The moon made her face bright and shiny, and her bright eyes were flashing.

"Why do you pay attention to that *Englischer?* What does he know? You've started saying silly things since he came to your house."

"Naw, I just wanted to make sure."

"About war?"

"No, about why we're going to be published and getting married." Now I wished I would have kept my mouth shut. I didn't want to hurt her or make her mad. But I just kept on going. "I just want to make sure we love each other."

"Was there any question before?"

"No."

"Then why should there be now?"

"I don't know," I said. "It was just a question I thought of."

We were quiet for a minute, and then she took ahold of my arm and asked, "Have I changed?"

I just shook my head as she looked at me and she continued, "Then who has?" She looked at me like one of the asters in our pasture. They're just as nice and blue as can be out there on the green grass but you snap them and puff, they're gone. They're stemmy strong flowers, but still if you twist them they'll wilt just like a delicate little daisy. No-siree-sir. I'd been stepping on too many flowers already, and it was time to shut my mouth.

I just looked down and felt sad. I looked at the yellow daisies on her light nightgown. *Ja*, she wasn't supposed to have something this bright, but this was a part of her. She was a large woman but all at once she seemed small under her soft gown. I just took my finger and touched the middle of her hand. It was kind of a strange thing, but it didn't matter because we looked right at each other, and I could see the bright light of her eyes.

But it came to me right then that she could be a blue aster when I was a good pasture. It was just one of those things you find out every now and then, and it makes you tired and happy just to think about it.

"It makes nothing out," I said. "And some time you can talk with Malcolm himself." I knew she thought I got all that stuff from him.

"Why?"

"Because you would like him. He's been to a lot of parts of the world. He's traveled to the West Coast and has lived in different places. Says he was a cowboy for a summer."

"Did he really?"

"Oh, *ja*. He's not a windbag like Toots," I said.

"Then why don't we do it?" She said it just like that.

"Huh?"

"*Ja*, don't you get bored around here? Do you know that I've never been out of Ohio?"

"Naw. It's different for us."

"Why?"

"We're different. We're better off here." I knew right then I had to talk some sense to her. "You don't want to go far away from here; otherwise you become dissatisfied. You have to think of the future; this is where we want to live and fit in. Some go away and they never can fit in again. What do you think happened to my brother Roy?"

She sat up. "But I'm not Roy. That isn't the same; you know that.

Wouldn't it be nice to go for a long trip, say to Yellowstone or Sarasota? Your cousin went to Australia and Germany for two years before he settled down. And even Chris was on a cattle boat for several years before he settled down."

I saw Bounce heading across the back-40, his short tail twitching, all geared up for a long trip. A red-tailed hawk could barely be seen as a wind current carried him away so that he went out of my view. "Wild," I said softly.

"What did you say?" She must have thought my gears had slipped.

"Oh, nothing important," I said. "But now I will say something and you listen to me. Forget everything I said about Malcolm and listen to me. He's different from us, and he moves around and doesn't have a home the way we do. This is our home and our people. It's better not to roam too much, not until we go on a honeymoon."

Anna sat up in the bed and looked at me that was like saying she really wanted to like me, but I knew I might as well have been talking to a log. She looked out the window and reached over and patted my hair, as if I were Bounce or something. I almost felt like barking at her or licking her face. She was quiet for a while and then she started in again on her faraway blue yonder.

"Ja, we'll go on a long trip on our honeymoon. Maybe we could even spend some time at Disneyland. Mullets went there, and they said it was so much fun."

I knew they were a bad influence on her when she did their housecleaning last winter. "Ja," I grunted.

"They showed pictures one night when I was there. You would have liked the wild west parts of Disneyland. I believe it must have been like that, all those Indians and buffalo; they even shot at them with arrows — just like Wild Bill Hickok. They saw fairies, giants and all kinds of Mickey Mouse people. They said it was the best trip they ever had."

"They're Mennonites."

She kept on looking out the window. The moon shown against the window and a light spot showed up on the dark polished floor. Little flecks seemed to move about in the air. They moved around like the little diamonds you can see in a kaleidoscope. They just kept going and going. But Anna kept her eyes on the outside and I could see the outline of her face as she moved closer to the window.

"Let's go outside." She whispered as if she didn't want to disturb anything. "The moon is full."

"*Ja.*"

She pulled the sheet back and grabbed my hand. "Come on, it's nicer outside."

"*Ja, vell,* I know," I said. "But what will your parents think if they find out we're out running around in the orchard at three o'clock in the morning? They'll think we've really gone nuts."

"*Ach vell,* it's just between us, and they won't find out anyway."

I stumbled around there for my pants and stepped in, pulling the suspenders over my shoulders. We tiptoed out the door and down the stairs. You'd a thought there was a fire or something the way Anna pulled on me.

In the living room at the front door I stopped and listened. The only thing I could hear was my breathing and Anna's. I pushed in on the door and turned the knob slowly. Click. I stopped and just held it, and Anna held on to my arm tightly. We were quiet for a minute and Anna pinched me in the rear. She giggled.

Then I heard stirring in the bedroom off to the side of the living room where we were. "*Vas geht?* Who goes?" Melvin's voice was sleepy and the bed springs creaked. Anna held on tighter and we just stood there as quiet as could be. It seemed like an hour had passed but then I finished the turn on the knob and pulled the door in. I pushed open the screen door, and Anna glided out.

I pulled the front door into the frame but didn't latch it. Sleep tight, Melvin and Clara, we won't disturb you further. I jumped off the porch. The wet grass tickled my feet.

Anna was standing in the middle of the front yard looking like some Catholic saint. Her body was outlined by the nightgown hanging loosely around her. I looked closely at her face that was outlined by her black hair. But it was bright. Her face shined like the face of one of those pictures of the Virgin Mary in the Bible stories we read as children. When *die Memm* used to read those to us when I was little, I wondered how a head could have that kind of a golden ring. Even the little boy Samuel had a halo in one of the books. Now it came to me. If you really loved someone, you saw them in the bright light of the sun or the moon and that put a halo on their heads. It was like they were holy to you.

We headed for the barn and the lane that went up to the orchard. The big farm collie came out of the barn and greeted us, but he didn't bark. He just sniffed and stuck his wet nose into our hands. The lane that went up through the trees was covered with grass with only some ruts where the wagon wheels went. I walked on the grass and Anna stepped on the bare tracks. Half the time I had no idea what I was stepping on, what with apples and peaches lying around. But then came the thistles.

"Ouch," I moaned as one of them pricked me right up in the big toe. I sat and held my toe up thinking I could pull the spine out. "Why did God make thistles anyway?"

Anna laughed, "Why not? Didn't you ever see how the gold-finches sit on them?"

"*Vell*, they can find some other place to sit."

"No, they eat some of those little white fuzzy hairs from them or use some of them for nests." She said this as if she knew something about them.

"*Vell*, I don't know that much about the goldfinches, but I do know these stupid thistles stick people and animals and choke out the corn and the hay. They're no good and the goldfinches can eat other things. Anyway, I need to get this one out of here." I kept trying to feel where the spine was in the toe.

"Here, let me doctor it," said Anna kneeling down and pulling the toe up to her face.

She looked closely at the big toe pulling it right up to her eye. She rubbed her forefinger lightly over the bottom of it. It tickled and stung when she touched the spine. I jerked.

She reached closely and pinched down in the toe. The little piece came out. I felt both pain and relief as the piece slid out. She held my foot and bussed the big toe with a hard smack.

"Now it'll get better," she said.

"*Ja, ja*." I laid back and laughed and still thought about thistles. "But why do we have the bad? Couldn't we just have the good things?" I felt the soft tickle and the sharpness of the place the thistle had been in my toe. "*Ja*, that's life. The tickle of the good and the sharp pain of the bad."

"But you don't really know anything about the bad," said Anna. "You've never had friends or relatives killed in a war. We've never been hungry. What do we know about evil? Can you imagine what it's really like to have problems?"

Now wait, I thought, here we go again on this how we don't know anything about the real world. Should we become like our ancestors who were chased all over the Old Country for their beliefs? They knew what evil was. "*Ja*," I said, "I know my life has been too good. It's much better than I ever deserve it. But we never know when things could get bad again. What should we do? Look for troubles?"

"No, I was just thinking you make too much of a little thistle."

"*Vell*, I'm thankful for the little things even. But what I really started to say was why God allows the bad things, not just if I have them. If God is good he shouldn't allow those things to happen."

I reached for a pear that was lying in the grass under the tree. Anna giggled. "*Ja*, that's the way it is." I handed it to her.

"That's all right," she said pushing it away. "You eat it."

I thought I'd say a little more, but the more I thought, the less I said. "What does it make out? If God wanted to give us some thistles and death, that's his business. He gave us a lot of good things too." I bit into the pear.

Anna put her hand on my chest and I forgot all about the questions. "Ach, who am I to ask so many things?" I said chewing the pear. I looked up at her head and again saw her halo. There was my saint again, and then she said the craziest thing.

"I'd like to go to Wheeling again."

I looked at her lips and thought I'd like to kiss you again. But I said, "*Ja*."

"I don't know. I'd just like to go before we get married."

I did know I wanted to pull her down on top of me. Judas, who cared about Wheeling?

"Your sister Leona would like to go too. And Sarah, maybe she'll go."

She smelled so fresh and I touched her warmth and she rubbed my chest. Her eyes were black but they seemed bright as little flashlights. What was she talking about? Wheeling. "*Ja*, sure go ahead," I said.

The halo came down closer to me, and the wet grass tickled my neck while she kissed my ear.

10.

The next Saturday night I went with the *Buwe* to Holmesberg again. We stood in small groups by our buggies behind the hitching post. With shining black shoes, pants freshly pressed and our navy bumper jackets, we looked pretty sporty. Everybody was washed and smelled good, and I combed my hair up in front like a little banty tail. We looked fine, really sporty.

The horses looked better on Saturday night too. We had them just freshly combed, and they were shining and snorting, ready to go. Flecha seemed to know when it was time for the *Buwe* and was ready to fly. She was the nicest horse in the whole bunch there at Holmesburg. She looked even better than I did.

Some of the *Buwe* went into Taylor's Tavern for a few beers, but I didn't. I wasn't much of a drinker, and I think a few of the *Buwe* who did, did it just to act big. Anyway, I couldn't see why someone would drink a lot of the stuff that tasted just like warm pee.

I went over to Wengert's Supermarket and got some things, and there was my buddy Mike. Mike had a car and we often went to Breman together where he dropped me off at Anna's, and then he went on to some girl down near Charm. Actually Mike was another one of Mony Hershbergers' boys. There were 13 of them and usually we just called them the Hershberger boys or the Hershberger girls.

He was eying the gum and the lifesavers. That was my job to keep him fixed up with them. "Here let me get you your supply."

"Ah, that's not necessary."

"*Ja*, but I'll get some anyway," I said, clapping him over the shoulder and taking some gum and lifesavers and a few fire balls, just for good measure. "You drive the car and I'll take care of the gum."

I bought some candy then and gave over half of it to Mike so he was nice and supplied. He bought himself a pack of Pall Malls and started in on baseball.

"You don't think Mickey can hit as many as Maris?" he asked.

"He's getting too old," I said.

"He's still quite a ball player."

"*Ja*, and the Yankees will win again this year."

"But they don't have the pitchers. You've gotta have the pitchers." He rubbed his hands over the baseball he had stuck through his radio aerial and then he wound up like a Sandy Koufax.

"Didya hear that game last Sunday between Cleveland and the White Sox?"

"*Barmlich*, I wish I could have seen Tito Francona hit that one in the left field stands. 'That ball is gone, gone, gone . . . for a home run.'" He sang it out just like a real baseball announcer. Boy, did he hold out that last g-o-n-e twirling it around like it was the first line of the "*Lobg' sang.*"

"*Ja*, the Indians can hit when they have a good day."

"But they haven't got the pitching."

"Their problem is they trade away the good hitters."

"Hitting my rearend, they don't have the pitching."

I knew I'd never get him off his pitching line, but I didn't like the trades Al Saul had made. "Where are Maris and Colavito?" I asked. "Al Saul trades away everything good, so you'd better have some pitching. I hear now he wants to trade Harvey Kuenn too. He's the best we have."

"I still say it's the pitching. Piss poor, you've gotta have the pitching or else you're sunk in the stretch."

"*Ja*, the pitching is important."

"You're darn tootin'. You can't win without the pitching. If you don't believe me look at Los Angeles over there in the National League. Where would they be without that little Koufax?" He was winding up for some more pitches beside his '55 Ford. Of course, I believed the pitching was important.

"*Ja, vell,*" I said. "It looks as if we don't get ready to go, we'll be pitching to ourselves."

The buggies were backing up from the rail, and the horses were pawing the blacktop, leaving little sparks flying. Flecha snorted with the rest, and I could feel her zip zing right through the reins. I looked over across the rest of the buggies and the bright lights made the white rings shine nicely in the dark night and on the dark bodies.

The wheels whined as we backed out together, and then we were off down the street. The clip-clop clatter of the shoes on the blacktop bounced along with the flick of the lights. You could see the buggy lights bobbing along in the night air. Flecha pulled for more rein, but I held her in. Actually, she could have outrun any horse in our district, but we stayed behind Eli Hershberger's rig.

We were heading for Chris's place. There was a party down at Sol Troyer's south of Breman, and a lot of the *Buwe* were going. We often left our rigs at Chris's on Saturday nights and took off from there with cars.

I looked up at the windows and saw three little heads sticking out. They were my little nephews; they had heard our clatter and always wanted to see what was going on. I could feel their eyes searching me out and looking inside the buggy. They were interested in the little light switches on the dashboard and wanted to know what time I'd come back in the morning.

We must have been quite a picture as we came to the lane. Each horse leaned his head sideways for the turn, blew some white steam in the fresh evening air and brought the buggy into the gravelly drive. Buster barked and the Muscovy ducks squawked as the steel rims clattered on the gravel stones. I knew what those young nephews were thinking. They were thinking of the day when they would be old enough to have a rig and a horse with a lean and fine dark head with bright eyes like Flecha.

I unhitched Flecha and tied her in the stable and went out to join Mike and his '55 Ford for Breman, and there's when I got a big surprise. Malcolm showed up. There he was with Leona in the front seat with him, looking all spiffy like she was going to some hillbilly concert at Wheeling. I just couldn't believe it. What was this *Englischer* doing coming by here with the car and then bringing my sister along like he was going on a date?

Good night. They must have gotten their screws loose that

evening because Leona was pretty levelheaded, and Malcolm never made any signs of putting the make on her. *Vell,* maybe he wasn't, but it still didn't make any sense for him to come over here like that with my sister. I was sure that she had snuck out of the house after Ben and *die Memm* had gone to bed. Judas, would the old man be mad when he heard of this.

Nobody else went close to that blue Plymouth, but I walked up to Malcolm's side. They had some nice music on, and Leona was looking down at the radio as if she could make it come out better, chewing gum like a heifer.

"What goes?" I asked.

"We thought maybe we'd go down to Sol Troyer's for the party."

"Uh huh," I grunted. I knew he must have talked this over with Leona because he wanted to know more of what was going on.

"How about going with us?" That's what Malcolm said. Judas, the guy had the gall to invite me to one of our own parties. This was nothing but trouble. I should have sent them home right then and given Leona a good tongue-lashing, but then I got good-natured and tried to think maybe it doesn't matter. *Ach vell,* let them go and find out for themselves. He wanted to know what a party was like; might as well find out.

Leona usually had more common sense about these things than I did, and she should have known better, but her brains were off in the wild blue yonder. *Vell,* let'm go; I knew he wasn't going to go off to some field and jump her.

I could have gone with them, but where would that leave Mike and Anna? Naw, let them go and we'll come down there with Mike. That was a mistake, of course, I know that now, but you don't always know these things before they happen.

"*Ja vell,* go on," I said. "I'll come later with Mike." Leona was looking down at the radio, but then she looked up at me, and her eyes said thank you. She had this nice yellow nylon scarf on and looked pretty spiffy. I even began to think they looked like a pretty nice pair. It's something the way your mind can let you go like that. They both had sharp noses and were quiet.

Vell, I let them go then and just thought nice thoughts and went over to Mike, and we were soon sailing down to Breman in the '55 Ford. Mike pulled one of his Pall Malls out of the pocket and puffed real dignified like he was some kind of a banker. I felt the fresh air come in at the open window and rested my head back on the seat. It was time for more baseball.

"Wish they'd let Piersall alone."

"*Ja*. I kinda like him too," I said. "But he seems to always be doing something. Did you hear last Saturday when he played just behind the second base for that Chicago pitcher."

"*Ja*, that pitcher, Wilhelm!" Mike whistled. "What a pitcher, what a pretty knuckle ball! That's the trouble with the Indians. We haven't got the pitching."

"Piersall can hit. Not the big homers, but he can hit."

"*Ja*, sure, he's all right, but you can't depend only on the bats. You've gotta have the pitching . . ."

I closed my eyes and smiled. The fresh air felt good. What if we only had Jimmy Piersall and Hoyt Wilhelm to worry about. I thought of Anna. She'll tiptoe down to the door when she hears the car. When she greets me, she'll throw her head slightly to the side. A few strands of hair will fall across the side of her face, and she'll look sly as a fox.

Mike had started off again on the pitching; I just threw in a line every now and then to keep him happy. "*Ja*, you're right Mike. The pitching."

Anna will be thinking places where she hasn't been and where we might visit. She'll remind me of how the Mullets have gone many places and how that Gravey Ben traveled all over before he settled down. She'll pump me full of questions on my one cousin's trip to Australia and how he spent over a year there with the aborigines and the kangaroos.

Mike was quiet and waiting so I threw him a line. "Should the Indians trade Jim Grant?" He liked Mudcat Grant so that kept him going for a while. I heard some cowbells in a meadow near Breman and thought of Benny and then Malcolm and then Leona. I knew it was a mistake not to send them right home from Chris's but sometimes you even let your friends make a mistake. And maybe they'd change their minds on the way.

"*Ja*, sure the White Sox have the best pitchers," I said to Mike.

We picked up Anna and she looked just as nice as I had pictured her. She had on a bright yellow nylon scarf like Leona's and the tail of it would flutter with the breeze which came in the window of the car. Mike turned up the music, and we just listened to some loud hillbillies as we drove along.

"Just look at my hands," she complained. "I had to help with the shocking all afternoon."

"*Ja*, they're red, but do they feel sore?"

"They do. Can you feel it?" She held them up to my face, and I held her swollen fingers and pictured my girlfriend out in the field this afternoon making wheat shocks.

"Maybe I can help you some day."

"Dad was worried that it would rain and even *die Memm* was out there helping to shock."

"*Vell,*" I said. "Sometimes we all have to work together."

"*Ja,* that's what Dad says." She looked down at her legs with red streaks from the wheat stubble. "But it does cost more for those of us who do not wear the pants."

I knew that her Father needed her more because he did not have any older sons. How she could be so strong and so much like a girl all at the same time was a strange thing to me, but she was. And then she got interested in the music.

"Did you hear more about the music show in Wheeling?" Her eyes were bright and longing, a little like Flecha before an evening run.

"*Ja,* I guess Roy and some are planning to go."

"And some of us girls are planning to go too."

"*Ja, vell,* if you get a big kick out of hillbilly music, why not? But I'm not interested in going with Roy."

There was a big crowd at the party: more *Buwe* and girls than you can shake a stick at. These people down here in these districts south of Millersville were pretty outlandish with their drinking and all, but everybody came to the parties. The lawn was full of people, and there was a nice mandolin and guitar duet that had the music floating around the trees.

Anna and I got separated after a while, and I went looking around. I'd say everybody and his uncle was there from all over Holmes County. That's when I dropped on Malcolm out at the barn. There was some giggling and rumbling and a crowd down at the bottom of the barn hill, and there on the bank was Malcolm and four *Buwe.* I stood there in the crowd, and the first words I could make out made me feel like pure dirt.

"I have a friend here," said Malcolm. His voice sounded nervous even though he was trying to be calm.

"A friend here. Good sir. I am your friend. You came to the right place." It was one of those half-drunk rearends who was probably really concerned about this *Englischer,* but he was also just putting on a show. Another one grabbed Malcolm's arm.

"It's an *Englische* calf all right," the show-off said. I think it was some Schrock fellow. "What do you want here?"

"I said I have a friend here. But mostly I would simply like to attend the party."

"So you have a friend at dis party, do you. *Vell* dat is downright fantastic dat you should have a friend here, and I think it is significant dat you have a friend here. So would you commence to tell us who dat might be? " There were a lot of giggles and laughs as he talked like this, real slow and clear. He was trying to sound like some kind of a college professor, but mostly he wanted to be funny.

But it wasn't all funny. Several weeks ago one of the *Englischer* town boys had hit a buggy with his car and then blamed the whole wreck on the *Buwe* and beat up one of *Buwe*. No-siree, this could turn bad.

Malcolm looked around. We were standing there below the hill, and did he see me? I'll never know. He could have said Leona too, but he knew better than that.

"No, I don't believe my friend is here," said Malcolm.

"No-siree, your friend is not here so you can look for something else to converse about," said the drunk boy.

"No, he's not here yet, but I brought his sister." He said it in a quick moment, and I probably should have stepped forward and stopped this, but I didn't.

"His sister. Here we have it," said the leader of the four drunks. There was no giggling now. "So you'd like a woman, uh? "

"No," answered Malcolm sharply.

"What would you like to do to her? "

"He came for one of our women," said another one in the group.

"I didn't say that."

"What would you like to do to her? Uh? Do a little of this? " The little drunk leader rocked his privates back and forth like a little bull, and I felt sick on my stomach. Why did I allow them to come down here? I should have saved him from this when I saw him back at Chris's.

"I want to go home please," said Malcolm trying to sound even-keeled but his voice was nervous.

"Oh please, please, we don't want you to go home. We want you right here." The leader grabbed Malcolm's chin and his small eyes were fastened onto Malcolm's face. I thought he looked like a snake the way his eyes were dangerous and mean.

"Yes, the Mister would like to see one of our women," said another of the Buwe.

Malcolm moved his head sharply and the young man's hand was shaken loose. "No, I don't want any of your women. I'm at the wrong place here, and I now realize that. I want to leave right now, so let go of my arm."

He jerked his arm sharply, got loose, turned around to go. The banty gave him a kick right in the rearend. That got another one of them bold, and he slugged him in the shoulder. Malcolm stumbled and almost fell, but he didn't go down and never turned around. They gave him two or three more cracks as he stumbled along out the lane.

Then the leader turned about halfway so that all of us could hear. "Bye, bye little calfie, and you come back again and see us, sometime when your girl friends are home." He then changed to that dignified dirt tone: "Yessirr Mister, it takes some intercate arrangements to prepare for these social endeavors. So the next time dat you come, we'll send you an invitation and you can respond R.S.V.P. and sank you very much."

Now there was a lot of loud laughing.

"Yessirr, R.S.V.P."

It happened so fast and it was terrible. Everybody else thought it was funny and mean.

I went back toward the house and found Anna. "Let's go home," I said and she seemed to know there was a problem. It took a while, but we found Leona and Mike and his girl, but they didn't want to go. So I was stuck.

I ran out the lane by myself and wanted to talk to Malcolm. I wanted to apologize. I wanted to tell him that if those drunks would have done more I would have defended him. But I couldn't find him. He had left. I went to the knoll by the lane and watched the crowd moving around. The guitars were playing and they were doing some lawn dancing, but it didn't mean a thing to me. I was thinking of how weak I was and how I could never do anything right.

It was one of the longest nights I ever had, and on the way home Mike couldn't stop talking about the fight. The way he talked about it you'd a thought it was a baseball game, even if it really wasn't a fight. I just let him rattle away at the mouth and sat between Leona and Anna like a defeated soldier.

Leona didn't say much, but she did thank me for letting her go to the party with Malcolm. No, I said, it was a mistake. I shouldn't have left you and him go. But she claimed that it was okay. Anna was quiet and held her arm tight around my shoulders all the way home. It was one of the nicest things she ever did for me.

11.

Malcolm left without a word. Early that morning when Leona and I got home in the buggy, we saw that the car was gone. Leona cried when we walked back to the shed where it used to be parked. It was the first that I really knew that she liked him.

"It just seems so quick," she said. "He was here for a few weeks; we'll probably never see him again."

I didn't say anything, but I just stood there feeling sad and angry. Sad, because I had betrayed this friend in not helping him at the party, and angry that he had hurt my sister. I knew he didn't mean to but he did anyway.

All his talk about not hunting, not hurting anyone, "humanitarian" and other fancy words was just so much horse manure when I saw my level-headed sister crying. Not that I wanted them to be in love or get married or anything like that, and any friendship can end like this. Anyway, Leona's since found a good Amish guy, but you don't have the whole picture in mind at these moments when someone is crying.

"*Vell*, he probably should never have come here and I should have put my foot down about the party," I said.

"No, it was better this way," she said and sniffled some more.

Vell, I left it like that, and we didn't bring it up much after that.

We didn't think much about Malcolm that week because we were busy as ants with the harvests and that same week Roy came back home again. He still had about three weeks left of his leave from the Air Force, before he'd go back down to Florida and all his rockets and missiles.

He seemed to be in a better mood, and most of the time he helped us on the farm. We were putting in a new hog barn and special farrowing stalls for the sows. Each sow was going to have her own little pen like a cow stanchion. Anyway, Roy liked this work better than in the fields.

I didn't say much when Roy came back. I didn't have anything against him when he left, and now that he came back I just wanted to get along with him. But actually I wanted to be his friend, too. To have some talks the way we used to when we were in grade school and discussed the teachers. Maybe I could understand him better, and he wouldn't think I'm such a stuck in the mud.

One afternoon we went crow hunting, and I thought we might talk about some things, but all we talked about was the crows and finding ginseng up in the woods. *Vell,* I just tried to tell myself that some people you're close to and some you're not. But it still made me feel sad sometimes that we were brothers and weren't friends. Judas, that sounds bad, but I think that's about it.

Benny was just jumping to see Roy. He liked everybody— Malcolm, Roy, Leona, Toots the milkman, Bounce, you name it— Benny got along with him. I kinda wished I would have been more like him. Roy would take him on fast rides with his new car. Oh *ja,* he came back with a '57 pink and white Ford Galaxie. "The little grasshopper has an appreciation for some things these other stuck-in-the-muds know nothing about," said Roy.

Die Memm was glad that she had helped him to buy the car when he left. She had tears in her eyes when he came back. I'm not sure if that was right or not, and I know Dad would have been even madder if he'd a known about it. Ben didn't talk to Roy the first few days, and he told me he still didn't know about the will. He'd already got more money out of the family than he was worth.

Chris liked to see Roy because it gave him another chance to try to convert him. One afternoon we went over to Chris's to help on the basement they were putting under one part of the house. We carried big rocks out of there, and Roy put on a nice little show for the nephews. *Vell,* he was strong as a bull. Then in the evening we went down to Sand Creek and threw rocks at the bullfrogs in the dead pools beside the creek.

I know Chris didn't like the influence of Roy on his boys, but it was the price he had to pay to have Roy there to convert him. He'd work on him with questions about whether he was right with God and if he ever thought of what would happen if he would die in his sleep. Or when we talked about traveling, Chris would think of what would happen to Roy if he died in a car wreck.

Roy seemed to know what was coming and claimed that he had peace with God; it's just the backward people here on the earth he had trouble with. It didn't make that much sense to me because Chris always told us that our problem was that we were too backward and didn't have education. *Vell,* Roy was out in the world and he wasn't backward, and it sure didn't make him any better.

But Chris said what Roy didn't get was moral training. That's what was needed. Yup, Ben never taught his children anything but the value of the dollar. No moral and spiritual training but just tradition, and no wonder the children turned out bad.

The same week Roy came back I got a letter from Malcolm. It was the first we'd heard from him since the Sol Troyer party. We talked about him a little but not much. It was as though it was important when he was here, but now just like that it was over. Ben wasn't even that mad when he found out that Leona had gone to the party at Sol Troyers with Malcolm. *Die Memm* and the rest of the family didn't want to hear anything of the Sol Troyer party and just remembered the good worker that he was. They just acted as if the going was expected.

Leona and I had our own feelings about it all, but we didn't talk much about it to the others. One thing Malcolm had left was his flashlight, and Benny carried it around all the time saying, *"Englischer"* and *"Schtadt gehe."* The little idiot helped us to admit it. The *Englischer* had gone to town.

On Saturday evening after dinner Roy and I went up to our room, and I showed him the letter.

Dear Wayne,

I'm sorry that I left so quickly, but I thought it best that I no longer stay. You probably heard about the unfortunate incident at the Sol Troyer place. I'm sorry for any embarrassment I may have caused you, and you can be certain that I have nothing but good memories of your family and its kindness to me. Please share this message with them.

Friend,
Malcolm

Roy handed it back to me and grunted. "He was a good man," I said.

"What did he want here anyway?"

"Huh? He never really said. *Vell,* I guess we never really asked."

"Why didn't you ask him?"

I looked out the window and thought of our times together. I tapped the letter on the desk. "He said he wanted to live with us. And he really did; you should have seen him make hay and thresh."

"I'll bet the old man liked him."

"They got along, *ja.*"

Roy leaned back on his bed trying to act relaxed like he knew so much. Judas, why was his attitude just as if I didn't know anything?

"But, see here," he said. "Did you know how to deal with him?"

"How do you mean?"

"Just that. What do you know about getting along with the *Englische?* You don't know why he came, and you don't know why he left. See, he was probably some news reporter or a detective. You don't know what all he was after, but it was no good and you better believe it."

He stopped talking for a little and then he started up again. "Did you make him pay for his room?"

"No."

"That's what I mean. Why not? Do I get to stay here for nothing?"

"He worked it out."

"Bull. How can some wet-behind-the-ears college kid help on a farm? The old man and you know nothing about how to deal with the *Englischer,* and you'd better believe it."

"He helped."

"What happened at Sols'?"

"He should never have gone there." I didn't want to say too much.

"Didn't you tell him to stay away? Good night, for some *Englischer* to go to a place like that alone."

"*Vell,* he wasn't alone; he went . . ." I almost told him about Leona, but then I caught the words. Anyway, Roy wanted to do the talking.

"*Vell,* until you get out of this back-end of the country and learn about the real world, I wouldn't take some no-count college student in the house. You don't know how to deal with them, and you'd better believe it."

"He was a good friend."

Roy put on his clothes and left for Holmesburg with his car. I followed about an hour later with the buggy. The clouds were dark and the air was heavy. Flecha was already covered with sweat by the time we got to the edge of town. There were Mike and the *Buwe*. We went through our usual things at Holmesburg, and Mike took me down to Anna's.

I was wet when she met me at the door. There she was with the hair falling over the one side of her face. Lively and sly and with a slight smile on her face; that's just the way she always looked with a little twitch on her lip and a bright light in the eye. It was as if she knew that there was something funny about the world.

She took my hand and we tiptoed upstairs and I took off my shoes. The lightning struck hard outside, and the rain was dripping on the roof. We listened to the sounds outside the open window and on the roof. A robin whistled some rain song between the thunder claps, and we could hear the water flowing on the roof as well as the drips. Anna had opened the attic door to make the sound clearer.

I wasn't frightened by the thunder and lightning and the rain, and I thought of the growing corn. The only bad thought I had during these times was of the stories that *die Memm* used to tell when we were little of the young man who was standing at the front door and struck by lightning. Struck dead. He was going to a picture show and that was his punishment. I think all the mothers in the district told that story because it helped the young ones to know how bad the picture shows were.

The clock struck one.

"Will Roy stay for a long time?" Anna asked.

"I don't know. He still has about two weeks left of his two-months furlough," I said.

"Is he better this time?"

"*Ja*, actually he gets along better with Dad this time."

There was another thunderclap.

"I sometimes wonder why he left us," I said.

"He wanted to see the world."

"But why can't he fit in when he comes back? Has the world made him better? What's wrong with our life here?"

"There's another large world out there, and we don't know anything about it."

"But why do we need to know anything about it? It's all evil anyway." I knew she was wondering how I knew. "Just look at the newspapers."

"But maybe we should know about the evil too."

"You've been watching too much TV over at the Mullets."

"No, don't you ever wish you could run away for several years and then come back here and live our life? "

"No." It wasn't quite true, but I said it quickly because she was getting crazy ideas.

"I do."

I just grunted and thought of how she goes nuts like this off and on. She'd be some hillbilly housewife, if I wouldn't be around to give her some order.

"Remember Erik and Ingir in Norway, the little people in Malaysia and all those other people we studied in geography. They live very differently, or what about Hank Bontrager." I had a notion to say that, *ja*, we should take a trip around the world, but let her go. She'll come back, but for now she was really traveling. Back to Hank. "He went down to Paraguay in PAX and you should see his slides. He even learned some Spanish and says he almost brought back an Indian wife from down there."

"*Ja*. Hank likes to brag."

"I know but it was good for him to go. He went like a dumb little boy nobody gave a hoot over, and now he has all this experience, and he works better."

"*Ja*."

"And he helped some people. They didn't have roads down there. Said he helped the Mennonites and the Indians."

"*Ja*, I know it was good." I could have told her that I thought Hank was still Hank, only now he was a big boy and had some South American Indian and Mennonite stories to tell, but it wouldn't have done any good. Anyway, I agreed that it was good for Hank and for the people he helped.

Plus he got to show his slides to all the Mennonites and even to some of the young people from one of the districts over by Breman. They were mission-minded and let him show slides one Saturday night in a garage. This woman should have been thinking more about canning and making her future husband happy, but here she was off in the blue yonder.

"*Ja*, sometimes I'm afraid I'll have lived my whole life here but not have known what I've accepted or rejected."

"*Ja*, you've said that to me before." Go on my little colt and think these thoughts. They make you jumpy and frisky, but do they really matter? Or are they just hot air? I wasn't going to argue.

"If we could try some other living we could really be sure our ways and traditions are the best."

"But they are — for us."

"I guess so too, but it would be better to find out by experience."

"*Ja*, like Roy." I paused to make this point. *Ja*, I will argue. "When people leave here they don't come back. Or they are all mixed up when they come back. Like Roy, *litterlich* and *verhuddled*, wild and mixed up.

The kerosene lamp fluttered when a strong breeze of air came in through the window. Anna's face flashed and she kept going. "Sometimes they go and often they are stricter than the ones who have never left. Take Gravey Ben. He was so wild and went down to Sarasota every winter. And during the second World War, he was in CPS out in California. They say he even had an English girl friend out there." Then the smiling quiver came to her lips and she whistled. "Now he's one of the strictest bishops in the county."

Then we were quiet for a while.

"It may even have been good for Leona."

"What? "

"The *Englischer.*"

"No."

"Yes, now she knows what it's like." I didn't push her anymore and she didin't say anymore, but it seemed to me that she and Leona knew something about that that I didn't. They knew that some of these experiences are good for you as long as you didn't get completely swept off your feet.

The lightning kept on flashing, but the thunder was not as loud as it rumbled lower. The rain kept a steady stream on the roof, and I hoped it would stop by Monday and dry off. Chris needed help so I was planning to go over to the Yoders to build fence and face a day of questions from those little critters.

I thought of the tall anchor roots for the green stalks. The rain gave life and strength to the plants to grow into tall plants and well filled with grain. We'd cut some and blow them into the silo and put more in the crib. Farming always brought me back to the right world.

"Have you heard anymore about next Saturday? "

"Not much."

"It will be something," she said. "We don't often get to the Wheeling Jamboree and this is our chance. This is next to the Grand Ole Opry."

"You go. You'll enjoy it; it's not that much for me."

"Your sister Leona wants to go."

"*Ja,* I know," I said. Then I said my real concern. "It's partly Roy. I'm not hard up to go with him."

"He's acting better, isn't he? "

"*Ja,* but that's a long drive. I've been down 250 to the Wheeling Downs — to see the races — and that's bad road."

"Then isn't it here, too? Of all the crooked hill roads, we have the worst."

"*Ja, vell.*" I knew she was set to go. "Do the folks know you're going? "

"They didn't say no. They just warned about drinking."

She brought her face close to mine and it seemed soft and gentle. She gripped my head in her hands. "Please go. I don't want to go by myself. It's not safe by myself."

She was a large woman but all at once she seemed small to me, and I knew I would have to go. Just last week she had held me when I betrayed the *Englischer,* and with Leona going, it was the only thing to do.

"*Ja,* I guess I'll go, even if I don't trust Roy too far."

"How often do you get to hear Chet Atkins? " she asked. "It will be something."

"*Vell,* I'd rather hear Hank Snow."

"No one can pick the guitar like Chet Atkins."

"Maybe not."

"I wish I had a record of him."

"*Ja,*" I said. She laid her head on my chest and her sharp black eyes looked out the dark window, and I knew she was dreaming of Wheeling and Sarasota and Disneyland and Yellowstone. The rain had stopped except for little spurts, and a rooster crowed.

12.

The next morning I woke up at Chris's. I went over there on Sunday evening after the chores and stayed for the night. We were often back and forth like that, and since Chris was going to go to a barn-raising up in Wayne County and also needed to make some fence, I went over there in the evening. Our helping each other started when the boys were little and Chris needed more help, and I'd go over more, but since then I just went like a friend. *Vell*, and Martha was my sister. Ben would sometimes growl about if we didn't have enough work around home, but I knew that it really didn't make anything out to him.

I woke the next morning to the tune of "Aden, Raymond, Matthew."

I jumped out of bed and went down where Chris was reading at the kitchen table and Martha was frying corn mush. I sat down and picked up a *Herald der Wahrheit* which was lying on the table. Chris was having his devotions and there was no use bothering him. After about five minutes Chris went to the upstairs door again and shouted up the winding stairs: "Aden, Raymond, Matthew."

Silence. The only sound was corn sizzling in the skillet.

"Aden, Raymond, Matthew! Breakfast."

"We're coming!" It was Aden's voice. He sounded far away and muffled as if he came from deep down under a comfort. I knew he was coming but not right away. He was the oldest of the Yoder boys and it was his birthright to set an example which he usually did in a good way. But his being the leader didn't mean he wasn't still a hard sleeper, and he didn't like to milk any better than the rest. But anyway, he was smart and I knew he'd get up when it was time.

Chris went back to reading the New Testament and I kept on the *Herald* with one eye on my pious brother-in-law and the other imagining Sarah. Why I should have thought of Sarah that morning I don't know, and it was bad because I saw her jumping on her bed without any clothes on. She'd fly up to the ceiling and just stay there for a while, and it was just my bad mind trying to make her into an angel or something. I'd get these pictures every now and then; it was just the devil tempting me. I looked over at my sister Martha and knew that she never had bad thoughts like that and I shouldn't either.

I looked over at Chris and he was totally meditating on the Gospel of John. How I wished I could be religious like him. He was the best read person in the district, and he really wasn't in that big of a hurry for the boys because it gave him more time to read. He'd read all the time and his little Moody books and tracts were all over. You'd find them on top of the two-by-fours in the backhouse or on the beams in the straw shed.

None of us wanted to talk about it, but we were afraid he might have wanted to become a minister. *Vell,* none of us talked about it but my dad Ben. Chris was in the lot several times, and Ben said that much reading does not a minister make, and he was glad that God didn't choose him.

Chris finished the chapter he was reading and went to the stairs again. "Aden, Raymond, Matthew, breakfast. Second call." The last words he kind of ran strung out in a friendly tune. "Come on, the cows are waiting." He looked over at me. "Wayne's here and waiting for you." Silence and then a pause. "I want some word that you're awake.

"Coming." it was Aden's voice again, just slightly stronger. "Yup, just hold on, we're coming," called Raymond. He was a favorite of Chris's. Like his father he didn't like the cows and would have liked to do more mechanical things. He was always building a hoopy or making some new toys. I expected him to get to the barn first, not because he liked the milking but because he wanted to get it over. He was also smart as a cookie, and his father liked him for that.

"We're coming," called Matthew at last. The third oldest, he called last and got to the barn last too, even if he liked the animals best. After he got there he stayed longest too. He was crazy about animals and was always trying to take chicks to bed with him or picking up stray puppies. Martha claimed that he would just as rather sleep in the barn even if they never let him do it.

Chris went back to reading and the boys kept on with their sleeping and peeing. They all peed in their beds like little spigots. It was something they got from the Weavers. We knew they'd stop soon enough when they got to the upper grades. *Die Memm* once took me to the family doctor to get little pills for it, and one time she even took me to *Brauch* Mart, but I just grew out of it.

"The car's coming at seven-thirty," said Martha. She put a cup of coffee in front of the Bible on the table. She was trying to tell him that we'd better get on with the chores if he's going to be ready for the car to go to the barn-raising. Chris went to the door again.

"Aden, Raymond, Matthew! Third call." There was a pause. "Corn mush, applesauce, ice cream." *Vell,* we weren't going to have ice cream for breakfast, but it was Chris's way of being real positive with his boys and he always claimed he wasn't tight like some of the others in the district.

He looked over at me and began a little speech on raising his boys. "*Ja,* if you treat them right they'll stick to you. I see over here how Mony Hershberger does it. He has them working out in the fields and fence rows from morning till dark, and all he has is a bunch of tubs who don't like him and would like to run away. I say we'll treat our boys right and they won't forget it." He looked over at Martha.

Martha nodded.

"*Ja,* I went over past Hershbergers last week and he had them all out there cleaning the fence row till it was pitch dark. You'd think the night was all a mistake. I say let them play some too and then they'll listen to you."

Martha nodded. Chris read a few more lines and then he went to the door. He stomped like a horse and clicked the latch. He threw all that positive stuff out the window just like that and got mad: "Aden! Raymond! Matthew! Last call! And I want to hear you on the floor or I'm coming up!"

He shouted and sounded just as growling as a mad dog. If a few minutes ago Jesus was blessing the children, this was Jesus cleansing the temple.

"Now, careful you don't wake little Samuel in our bedroom," said Martha.

"*Ja,* I'm having trouble getting these pants on," Aden responded.

"Nothing doing of that anymore. I want to hear feet on the floor and a word from the rest," Chris growled back.

"*Ja,* coming," It was Matthew's sleepy voice.

"Raymond, do you hear me?"

"*Jaaaaa!*" Raymond shouted loud enough that the cows should have heard him. "Do you think I'm deaf? Now let me get my shoes on."

We heard some feet shuffling on the floor and that was enough to let us know they'd soon be down, and we'd soon be out milking.

After breakfast, Chris read another chapter from the Bible, but I had trouble paying attention. Sarah came back on my brain. I often did that when there was something religious going on like church or reading the Bible or devotions like this. Sarah was such a dainty little Jersey and she had such sharp features and I thought of lying flat on my back and seeing her naked little body floating up there in the ceiling. It was terrible, and I shouldn't have done it; anyway, Sarah was Anna's friend, and you shouldn't do things like that to a friend but the thought came anyway.

I looked at my little nephews who were snuggled up to each other near Martha. My sister sat silently giving close attention, but at the same time she seemed relaxed. "The next day he saw Jesus coming toward him, and said: 'Behold the lamb of God, who takes away the sin of the world.'" Chris read the words as though they were important, but not in the holy singsong way the ministers read at church. Sarah's sharp eyes flashed at me, but she was innocent. She couldn't help it if I lusted after her.

"Then if we are united, let us pray," said Chris, and we all fell to our knees. "Holy God our Father, we are thankful that thou hast given us another day. Thou who makest the heaven and the earth . . ." And he went on like this.

I looked over and saw Aden pinching Matthew's toe. My eye strayed to the side and there was Martha's rump turned toward me. It was large and pure and covered with her blue dress, but it changed into Sarah's white rump and back, smooth and twitching in the morning air. I wanted to thank God for such a beautiful creature, but I also felt like the dirtiest pile of manure. What would my good pure sister think if she knew my dirty thoughts. Or my little nephews?

I tried to listen to Chris. "And forgive us where we have failed and for those who have departed from thy true path." We knew who he was praying for. "We pray that thou wilt chasten and bring them back to the right way which thou hast said is straight and narrow."

The prayer was broken into with the roar of the milk truck. Toots was driving in at Bush Mike's Mart's lane and now was heading up the hollow. I should have prayed for Toots; he needed God's help. I could see him heading up the lane, bumping along on the front seat with a cigarette sticking out the front like a little missile that he could aim in any direction. I don't think I've ever seen Toots without a cigarette. He'd smoke so many he'd buy them in the carton, and we'd see the cartons lying on the seat of the truck cab.

Ja, God help Toots and his wife and may we be thankful for the good families we have. Toots and his wife fought every day, the neighbors said. There was a little hole in the back of his truck about the size of a pipe. Everyone said that hole was where Toots's wife had rammed a pipe that was originally aimed for Toots's head. Judas, here I was thinking of naked women, and I should be praying for men and women who are fighting each other with pipes.

"May we be true to thee in all that we say and do." Ja, Christ, I feel guilty for the thoughts about Sarah. Why did I do these things? I'd seen women without any clothes on and it's all right. It's just when I think of these things when they have their clothes on that it's bad. I must be more careful, I prayed.

"And so we join in praying as thou hast taught us, 'Our Father which are in heaven, hallowed be thy name.'" Chris said the Lord's Prayer so sincerely and with expression that I thought he could have written it himself.

Aden ran out to the barn right after the prayer, and Chris left for Holmesburg to catch a carload that was going to the barn-raising up in Wayne County. I soon headed for the shed and the fencemaking tools.

Toots's truck came roaring in Chris's lane. Toots never had a muffler on his truck, and you could hear it a mile away. When it was close, it really boomed. He shifted down and there were some loud pops as it settled to a stop in front of the barn. I glanced over and saw Aden running from the haymow to the front of the barn. I found out later what all that racing around was about, but at the time I didn't pay much attention to him. We heard the cans clanging together as Toots hoisted them over his back. Buster barked, and the ducks squawked and then Toots was roaring out the drive.

That forenoon we got a lot of fence fixed, and everyone worked so good I knew there was something the matter. Then after lunch I found out why Aden had been so nice and why he had run out of the house like a dog after a bone. He had snitched some cigarettes from the front seat of Toots's truck in the morning. After lunch we just got back to the fence when Aden pulled a new pack of Pall Malls out of his pocket and said to his brothers, "Did you ever see these before?"

"Where did you get them?" asked Matthew.

"I'll bet you took them from Toots's truck," said Raymond.

"Why did you do it?"

"Come on, I thought you'd want to try a little smoke." Aden looked at me really sheepishly to see what I would do about it. That's when I should have put my foot down right then and told the little rascal to give the cigarettes back to Toots in the morning. But I let them go. They're good boys and if they want to try something dumb like this and take a smoke, let'um go.

I just kind of looked out in the wild blue yonder and played possum, and it didn't take Aden long to go ahead with this smoke game.

"You aren't afraid to take a little puff? Are you? Now, let's see. Who hasn't smoked yet? Is it your turn?" He turned to Matthew and tipped over the pack of Pall Malls. He popped the pack up and down on the flat of his hand until one of them came out, and then he really finely picked it up just the way he had seen Toots do it.

Matthew took the tobacco in his hand and held it like some little garter snake. "Why don't you smoke it yourself?"

"I will, sure," said Aden. "But we want to make sure you learn. You can do it."

"Ja," said Raymond. "It's about time you learned how to smoke."

Matthew put the tip into his mouth, the end sticking up in the air like a little smokestack and Aden struck a match. "Now when I hold it to the cigarette, you breathe in, understand. Isn't that the way you do it?" he said looking at me. Little rascal, he knew that I didn't smoke cigarettes. He'd probably only smoked once or twice himself, but here he really wanted to be the big shot.

Matthew sucked in his breath. He took the cigarette out of his mouth and blew out a short puff that made nice little white clouds in front of us. "Not bad," said Aden.

"Yep, you're doing nicely," said Raymond.

Matthew got a little more confidence, and he coughed like he was important and took a few more puffs. He even put his mouth in a kind of sideways angle, blowing the smoke in little puffs out of the side of his mouth the way he had seen Toots. It crossed my mind of how Chris would feel with his little boys out here puffing away.

The other boys also lit up and took short puffs. Aden tried to give me one. "Naw, you know I don't smoke those little ones." Actually it was true. I didn't smoke cigarettes even if I sometimes smoked a cigar, just the way Chris and some of the other men from our district did. A lot of the *Buwe* like Mike Hershberger smoked them all the time when they were running around and stuff, but I never liked them.

The boys kicked against the fence posts and coughed. They flipped the ashes off with their little fingers, just the way Toots did. The smoke went curling up into the clear sky, and you would have thought there was some Indian powwow going on.

"Now you're catching on to the real smoking," said Aden. "You've only got one more step. You've got to learn to blow through your nose."

"Here, I'll show you," said Raymond. "You suck in, understand. For a long time and hold it down. Then blow it out, but keep your mouth shut this time, so the smokes comes out of the nose holes." Judas, the little smart alecks thought they were really the experts after one cigarette.

"*Ja*, it's not hard," said Aden.

Matthew blew out a long breath of air, put the cigarette in his mouth and drew in a long breath. He must have sucked in for a half a minute; then he held his mouth closed and held out the little cigarette. His cheeks were bulging and then he began to sway.

"Now," shouted Aden. "Now, lift it up through your nose!"

But that was the end of the show. The cigarette fell from Matthew's hand and he fell flat down like a rag with the smoke curling gently from his mouth. Nothing was still coming from the nose.

I quickly picked him up and Raymond and Aden thumped him on the back. He coughed and sputtered like some little Briggs and Stratton, but at least he was showing signs of life.

"Why didn't you listen to us?" Raymond scolded.

Aden: "Through the nose, we said, through the nose."

Raymond: "Let's get him to the water trough."

Aden: "*Ja*, next time listen, dummy! We told you — through the nose."

"Shut up!" I said to the little bastards. I felt like whipping them and hanging them from the barbed wire and letting the crows peck at them. "You're the ones who got him into this. Don't you have any shame? What will Chris and Martha say to this? And that pack you stole from Toots's truck seat. I want a new pack put right back where you got this one — and by tomorrow morning."

I picked up the little boy and threw him over my shoulders, and we headed back for the barn, going in the back side where Martha wouldn't see us. I felt like we were coming home from a war that we had lost. The boys were quiet and I felt terrible because I wasn't a good influence on my little nephews, and I had thought of a naked woman this morning and that was probably what got us off on the wrong foot all day.

By the time we got to the barn, Matthew was all right, but we threw water over him anyway. The boys all gulped down water and tried to gargle to clean their throats. We went back then to the field, and before we put in the next post, we threw the pack of cigarettes, stubs and everything down in the bottom of the hole.

The sun was hot and we pulled the barbed wire tight and made the holes deep. If we did some bad, at least we made some good fence. I felt guilty that I had done something wrong to Chris and Martha because they didn't want little smokers, and I'd left them do it right in front of my eyes. Maybe they even did it because I was there. Why did they want to be like Toots and not me?

In about an hour Martha and little Samuel came with some lemonade, and I could have jumped down into one of the postholes myself. If those little boys didn't smell like a smoked ham, I don't know what did. She came right up to them and looked especially closely at Matthew. Aden all the time tried to keep a good conversation going on the lemonade, the fencemaking and the milking in the evening. Little Samuel even said, "Mam, who's been smoking?"

Before she left, Martha looked me right in the eyes and said: "Everything going all right?"

"Yup," I said. "We're getting it up and we'll be finished by five." I wanted to run after my sister and hug her when she turned to go. Little Samuel, grabbed her dress and said so we could all hear, "*Memm*, couldn't you smell, they were smoking?" They marched off, and we went back to work and were quiet for a while.

Then Matthew said it out loud, just like that: "It's in our breeding."

"What's in our breeding?" asked Raymond.

"To do bad. Look what happened to Roy. See, he used to do these things too. Now what kind of person is he? *Verrucht* and *litterlich*. Crazy and wild. Why do you think Horse Manuel studies the pedigrees? To see if the colts will amount to anything. That's why."

I felt bad for the little boy. He must have had this on his mind all afternoon, and maybe it would have been better if Martha had spanked him, but he was suffering enough and had to talk.

"You can't pick out just one person like that," said Aden.

"I'm not. We've got bad bloodlines. There's Daniel Schlabach. Where's he today? In the nuthouse. Don't you ever think of that?"

"Not often."

"I do," said the little guilty boy. Judas, *vell* I felt like Judas, for having betrayed that litte nephew.

"You shouldn't," said Aden trying to comfort him. "Don't just pick out a few bad apples."

"And Dad's a little crazy too."

"He's not!" The two older brothers said it together and then Aden went on. "He's all right. These things are not breeding. Now listen to me. Daniel Schlabach is not related to us. If he would have married Elizabeth, he would still only have been related by marriage. I told you that over at the pond the other Sunday, but you can't get it into your skull. We don't have his breeding. Anyway, even if we did, you can't just go on that. Even Horse Manual can't make them all turn out right. We might get a few bad ones, but the main breeding is good.

"Isn't that right, Wayne?" He turned to me for help.

"*Ja*," I said. "You're explaining it all right."

Aden marked an R on the fresh dirt with his toe. "Okay, Roy. He's just one. Look at Grandpa and Grandma and Wayne and Leona and John. And *Memm*. They're all okay; they're regular. Benny isn't quite all there, but he was born that way. Those things just happen if God makes us."

He continued, "Dad is not quite usual but he's not crazy. See, there's a difference. Everyone is different and he's a little more different, but he's not crazy. Do you understand that? So you're not crazy either. Is he, Wayne?"

"Nope," I said. "Aden is telling you the truth." Aden was trying to make up for all his mischief, but I wanted to back him up anyway and help my little nephew. I didn't know much more to say because I felt bad too that I had let this happen, and I knew Chris would really be disappointed if he found out. Anyway, I shouldn't have been thinking of Sarah the way I did this morning.

That's what started it all.

We worked hard then and just before the last staple went in Aden came to me and asked if he could run over to town and pick up a pack of Pall Malls before the store closed. He said he had some money and wanted to get them. I told him to go and get back soon.

When we got back to the barn Martha was already out getting started with the feeding. Raymond and Matthew didn't go close to her, but they were interested in their work. Martha looked so honest and good that I have never seen anyone as a better sister.

"Isn't Aden back yet?" she asked.

"No, he went over to town, but he'll be here pretty quick."

"Will the pack be put back in Toots's truck?" she asked.

What! I didn't think I really heard her. "What, what did you say?"

And she repeated it: "Will the pack be put back in Toots's truck?"

"Yup," I said. "That's what he went to get." She just stood there and looked sad; then I quickly added, "They won't do it again."

"I'm glad you were with them." That was all she said, and we went back to feeding and milking.

I never changed from feeling so bad to feeling better so quickly in my life. I watched her all evening as if she were some kind of saint who knew just what to do that was kind and right. She never said a word about it at all since that time, nothing that evening at dinner or ever. She even acted kind of cheerful and paid no attention to the boys' nervousness and lack of appetite.

Chris still was not back from the barn-raising when I left after supper. The sun was a golden yellow ball in the west behind the house, and Martha and the boys stood in the doorway and waved goodbye. For a moment I saw a golden ring around my sister's head, but then Flecha whinnied, and I was out the lane.

But I thought of her all the way going home. I don't think she said anything to Chris, ever. I never even figured out how she knew everything. What a woman my sister was. Loyal and true and only wanting the best for her sons. I couldn't think of one thing she had ever done that was really wrong. She always knew almost by instinct what was the right thing and then she'd do it.

Flecha blew like a steam engine and pulled for more rein. Nope, my little nephews didn't need to worry about their breeding. They had a thoroughbred for a mother.

13.

That Saturday was the music show at Wheeling. Roy, Leona, Anna, Sarah (may God dress her), Jonas Hershberger and I went. Jonas or Joni was one of the 13 in Mony's tribe, and he was a brother to baseball Mike, just 13 times as smart.

We were really dressed up for the show. The girls were all spiffy with little bright colored silk scarves and colored homemade dresses. Their hair was set with big waves in front and they smelled like something right out of a perfume bottle. They must have taken baths in perfume.

We looked sporty too. Jonas and I wore our navy blue bumper jackets, and I had on my matching blue Sunday pants and Jonas had English store pants. Roy had on shiny light green pants and a bright blue jacket over a flowered Hawaiian shirt that he had bought in Florida. His hair was wet and greased in a tight wad around his head, swirling into a duck tail in back. In front his hair was combed up in a sharp little curl. He looked like Hollywood.

"Who cut your hair, Joni?" Roy asked. "Looks like some calf was grazing on the edges."

"*Die Memm* did it."

"Why don't you go to a barber shop? Get them cut right, know what I mean? See, they know more about cutting hair than your old woman."

"*Ja.*"

"Sure, they cut them in the latest styles. Like mine. This is a duck tail. The hair is all thrown around to end at a point in the back . . . like a duck's rearend. Get it?"

Jonas laughed and the girls giggled in the back seat. I was crowded between Roy and Jonas in the front, and I looked closely at the wet grease of my brother's hair. I knew I was in for another of his Elvis hair talks.

"Came from Presley — Elvis — the one who sang 'Hound Dog' and 'It's Now or Never' and all those swift songs. *Ja,* he started wearing these slick pants and this haircut, and everyone soon caught on because they look good and everyone knows it."

Jonas just grunted but you could tell he wasn't believing all that baloney.

"So the next time the old woman wants to give you a haircut, tell her to give you a duck tail."

"Naw."

"You don't like it?"

"*Ja,* it's all right. But I don't want one for me."

"Yessirr, if you want to stay 100 years behind the times and look like something right out of the brush, that's your business, but I've been around. I know what other people do and what looks nice, and you'd better believe it."

"Roy, turn up that music." It was Leona in the back seat and she wanted to hear Tex Ritter sing. Roy reached down and turned it up and then reached up and slicked his hair back on each side and kept on talking a little louder.

"Did I tell you about the high school diploma I got in the Army?"

I said that I knew he had one.

"That sheepskin means that you're an educated person."

"*Ja.*"

"The way to get ahead in this world is through education. You can't be a dummy any more. What we need are schools, more schools and good ones. That's the trouble with the natives. They don't go to school enough."

"I guess it helps," I said. Why argue with him. He thinks he knows everything and just wants to blow off.

"You'd better believe it. I had to do a lot of studying about American history and science, even psychology. I'll tell you boy, those were courses where we learned some things, not this little add and subtract baby poop Fred Smith taught us at Holmesburg."

"I liked Smith and I learned a lot," said Jonas.

"Well, I did too, but see I didn't learn the things I got in high school."

"Our county scores showed pretty good." Jonas looked at me to back him up. "Remember Elizabeth Miller. Her brother Solly was in my class, and he rated in the 99th percentile in all the mathematics scores in the state." I nodded. Judas, who could forget Solly. He was smart as a whip.

"But I mean psychology. You don't even know what it is, but it's important and you'd better believe it. They study how you think and things about your personality. What you'd really like to do and what you finally do, because of people like the old man."

He stopped a little bit when two deer jumped across the road and disappeared in a gulley down below. We were still then and watched them go.

"This is where I need a thirtyautsix. Did you ever hear of Freud?"

"*Ja*," I said. "It's what I feel right now when I'm feeling good and happy like those deer."

"Naw, that's just your dumb *Deitsch*. This was a very intelligent person, Sigmund Freud. See, he was the man who figured this all out. He said part of us wants to be like an animal, to do what is fun, like those deer. The other part is our conscience; that's what we're supposed to do, according to the old man. But we can't act like either so we do the in-between thing. That's called the ego."

I nodded.

"It's very important."

"Sure enough," said Jonas.

"You can't get along with people and understand yourself unless you know these things. That's the trouble with the natives; they don't know what they need to get along in the world. And you'd better believe it."

"*Ja*," I said. "For your world you probably need it. But for our world, you have to only know the important things and on-the-job training. A lot of people know what the book says, but they don't know how to farm or do carpentry work. I didn't learn how to make fence in school."

"Who wants to do that all his life?"

"I don't think our life is that bad," I said. It was all I could say. Underneath I wanted to say that, *ja*, maybe we couldn't do anything but farm and building. And some time I'd like to leave too and try some other things.

Jonas put his head up on the dash and listened closely to the words. "I wish we could hear better back here," said Leona and we kept our mouths shut. I looked back at Anna and she was smiling. Was she with me or with Roy in our talk? I don't think she even heard half of it; she was so happy and her eyes were sparkling like the water of Tappan Dam we were passing.

At the Jamboree we found the girls buying trinkets after going to the toilets.

"Look at those natives. You could spot them ten miles away," said Roy. *Ja*, he's right, I thought, but why make such a big thing of it? Leona, Anna and Sarah didn't pay any attention to how different they looked from the others, and they were really caught up with the music and the atmosphere.

The girls bought silk scarves that had "Wheeling Jamboree" printed in big letters on them and flowers and guitars. I found out later that Anna had bought me a big handkerchief with bright colored flowers in the one corner and the name "Wheeling Jamboree." I still have it as a keepsake from that night.

Roy bought a cup that had a picture on it with bright red lips and printed below, "Hot kissin' from the Wheeling Jamboree."

Then we went in to the music. It was even better than I thought it would be and loudspeakers made the music loud and clear. I sat between Anna and Jonas and both of them would punch me when it was really good. My ribs took a big beating that night because they really liked it. The first two singers were the Cheney Brothers, and Jonas said they weren't as good as they should have been. He said the voices and the instruments weren't really together as one piece.

Jonas was a musician himself and a good one, and he knew what he was talking about. They didn't blend together the way you really wanted that, and the high tenor sang too much by himself. In between the singers there were radio advertisements for things like Wrigleys' Chewing Gum and Aunt Margaret's Oleo.

But whatever we thought of the Cheney Brothers, and they were just some hillbilly group I hadn't heard of before, we all liked Chet Atkins when he came on stage. He was the main thing of the evening, and when he came out there everyone knew it was going to be the best. He knew it too and when he waved to the crowd, it was a kind of now-you've-heard-the-others-and-you're-ready-for-what-you-really-came-for wave. We all clapped like thunder.

Chet Atkins was a little older than he looked in the picture Anna had shown me of him. She kept one of him all young and neat in her dresser, even signed by him. But who cared about his looks when he started to play. He had us all in a musical fairyland with his fast fingers and beautiful melodies. His fingers flew over the neck of the guitar like a spring warbler and out of those strings and the hollow wood came a sound as clear and as sweet as a nightingale.

When he played the "Orange Blossom Special," building up from a slow beat to a swooshing sound of flying fingers and a whistling train speeding away, we all clapped hard and Anna punched me so hard in the ribs I thought I'd lose my breath. I looked at her intent face and saw how the music was going right into her body and soul.

Anna was in a trance over that music. I watched her during the rest of the program as much as I did Chet Atkins, and I could see why she wanted to come so much. The muscles in her arms seemed to be tight as could be, and at the same time her face was relaxed with her lips quivering in a smile. Her eyes were fixed on Chet Atkins, and when she looked at me at the end of the performance, she was one happy and contented woman.

She squeezed my hand. I believe it was just that she wanted me to be with her at the concert. Jonas liked the concert because he thought of how he could play better himself. I was there mostly because of Anna and I do like to see that kind of thing, but Anna was there for the music.

On the way home she showed me the record she had bought of Chet Atkins and whispered that she hoped we could listen to it sometime together. "I can't wait to hear this record," she said. I knew we wouldn't hear it very often, but it was a nice thought anyway.

"I should have bought one too," said Leona wishing as we often do afterwards to hold on to something.

"I wish I could pick the guitar like that Chet Atkins," said Jonas.

"Wasn't he something?" said Sarah.

"Tree-mendous," said Jonas. "First rate guitar."

"Not as good as usual," said Roy.

"Come on, you know he was good," said Jonas.

"Nosirree."

"As though you would know."

"You'd better believe it. The other time I heard him the people started to clap a lot sooner on the 'Orange Blossom Special.' Tonight they didn't do it as soon."

"What does that prove?"

"That he wasn't as good. If the audience doesn't clap as quick or as hard, then he's not as good." Roy stomped his feet on the high beam switch.

"Bastards, why don't you dim?" he growled, and the other car finally dimmed.

"*Ja*, see, that's how you can always tell how a concert is going; you can tell how they clap, you'd better believe it." He paused. "Haven't you ever been to a show before?"

"I thought he was good," said Jonas. "What did you think, Wayne?"

I was getting sleepy. "Huh?"

"What did you think of Chet Atkins?"

"The best, really sharp." I closed my eyes and remembered, *vell* not the clapping, but the way Anna had hit me in the ribs. Sure he was good.

Roy stopped at a tavern near Cadiz, and we *Buwe* went in and had a beer and bought some potato chips and soda pop for the girls. Roy came out singing "Are you mine?" He pretended to have a guitar in his arms and he moved around just like Elvis Presley and singing to his girl. Jonas and I danced with him in what must have looked like a circus.

"Are you mine?" asked Roy.

"Yes I am," sang Jonas and I.

"All the time?"

"Yessireee." We held it out real nicely. Jonas even hit a harmony in tenor.

"All my own . . ."

"Here you are sweethearts, all the food you can gulp." Roy handed the food to the young women and started up the 1957 Galaxie. It purred like a big tomcat. "Listen to that *Buwe*. Finest car in Holmesburg." He threw a nice spread of gravel stones over the parking lot of the tavern. "That will help them to remember us," he said as though it were a secret, and we headed back up 250.

"Did I tell you about the time they clocked me at 90 on the outskirts of Canton?"

"Naw," Jonas was sleepy, and I didn't answer. I had one beer and its bad taste made me drowsy.

But Roy was feeling good now, and he told us stories of how he was smarter and could go faster than the police, only he usually called them "the fuzz." He told us about the fish in Korea, and the last I remembered he got onto psychology and explaining how important a high school education was. I would just nod my head off and on, and occasionally looked over at the speedometer that was moving between 40 and 80 as we wound around the hills.

I thought of the deer we had seen along the road, wondering where they would be in the middle of the night like this. They wouldn't be too far away because these deer don't roam more than a mile. And I thought of wild turkeys roosting in the low trees. Smart birds, settling down here in these hills in southern Ohio where there's not as much good farmland and more trees.

The girls were quiet after eating their refreshments. Leona would yell if the music wasn't turned loud enough on the radio. Jonas had even stopped disagreeing with the things Roy was saying and would just say, "*Ja*," or something half-baked like "you-bet-chour-boots." I think he was thinking of the music and how he would sometime pluck the guitar like Chet Atkins.

I drowsed off a little and when I opened my eyes again we had left the sharp curves of the road near Wheeling and were on the straight stretches near the Tappan Dam lakes. I looked at the peaceful waters of the Tappan Dam and thought of how gentle the earth could be. The moon reflected on the lake, and shining silver ripples could be seen where the breeze moved over the water. I glanced at the speedometer and Roy was coasting along at 75 miles an hour, and he had finally stopped talking. There was just the music.

In the back the girls were asleep and their bodies were hanging over each other like sacks of feed. Anna was leaning against Sarah but her head was up and she would nod to the one side and then the other. Was she dreaming about her Chet Atkins record? Maybe she was thinking of a trip out West when we'd go through the parks or up to Niagara Falls. Was she dreaming of some Sunday morning, driving up the lane where church is being held, sitting beside me with a little one on her lap and Flecha stepping like a royal coach horse? Her lips quivered even as her mouth opened in her sleep. That picture of her being my wild and my gentle one will always be in my mind.

I turned my face to the front window on the side and put my nose against it and breathed. The cool window steamed up and everything became dim and in outlines. The moon was now just a blurred image on the peaceful waters.

That was the last I remember of the trip before the accident. Near Urichsville, the road had a curve and it wasn't even that terribly sharp but we went straight ahead. I felt the brake and we were slammed around, so Roy must have been awake at least at the last moment, but it was too late and the car went tumbling down over the hillside below. It all happened in a split second.

I heard voices crying and sniffling, and I put my hand to my face and felt it wet with blood. My arms hurt, but my mind was clear. The car was lying on the side and Jonas was lying on top of me. He was conscious too.

"Try to get out," I whispered to Jonas.

"*Ja.*"

He *scrinched* around there and kind of stepped on me, but finally he pushed the door open and crawled out the top. I tried to look who was in back and see what was going on there, and I could see Leona's head at the bottom of the seat. "Are you there, Leona?" I said. "And what about Sarah and Anna?"

I could hear Sarah crying, poor girl. She said her side hurt so much. "Sarah's here but I don't know where Anna is," said Leona. I told them to wait, and Jonas and I would be back to get them out as soon as we found the others and flagged someone down for help.

Jonas held the door open as I crawled out the top. The car seemed top-heavy and creaked and moved, and I thought it might fall. But we jumped off and tried to find our way among the saplings and underbrush that was around the car and up toward the road.

"Anna, *wo bist du?*" I screamed as I headed up toward the road. And then we found Roy trying to sit up in the track where his Galaxy had struck down the brush and small trees. He had blood running down his sleeve and moaned, and I couldn't make out what he was saying. But he looked just like some big bulldog that had lost a fight, and I was sorry for him.

We left him and kept calling, "Anna, *wo bist du?*"

We went all the way to the road and I told Jonas just to stay there and flag down the next car, and then I doubled back down toward the wrecked car. Roy was stumbling around now with his dizziness and being half drunk he wasn't much help. I went down below the car and there off to the one side was a body lying in the weeds and briars. The one leg was bent way out to the side so that it must have been snapped. I ran next to her and stomped down some weeds and bent down over her. The face was lying on the side and it was pale and still. Her lower lip didn't quiver and her eyes were closed. She still had her light pink silk scarf on.

I whispered in her ear, "Anna, answer me. Anna, answer me." But there was no answer.

I put my head on her dead body and cried. There was nothing else to do; it was all over. The wages of sin is death, but I kept on crying and hoping in some way that life could come back to this dead body that I loved. I stayed there until Jonas came down again and said that an ambulance was coming, and he'd go see what he could do about Sarah and Leona.

He had tears in his eyes, and he just stood there looking down at us for a few minutes when he saw that Anna was dead. We were quiet except for our crying, but I'll always be close to Jonas for standing with me and not saying anything at that terrible moment. I know it was just by accident that Jonas and I were together, but he helped me to feel that I could take the terrible and the tender together.

The next Monday the *Daily Journal* carried the story on the front page and I looked at the picture of the smashed 1957 Ford Galaxy lying on the side. The line underneath the picture said it was pink and white. I read the story: "One Killed and Three Injured as Local Amish Youths Crash."

"Early Sunday morning a car driven by Roy R. Weaver lost control at a curve on U.S. Route 250 south of Urichsville and killed one passenger as it rolled over several times going down a small embankment. Anna Hostetler, 21, of RD 5 Millersville was pronounced dead on arrival at the Henry J. Claybourne Hospital in Dover.

"Three other youths were injured in the fatal crash and are still in the hospital. Sarah Hostetler, also of RD 5, Millersville, was transferred to an intensive care unit at the Columbus University Hospital Sunday afternoon because of extensive internal bleeding. She is listed in critical condition.

"The driver, Roy R. Weaver, 22, suffered a broken leg, but is listed in satisfactory condition. Leona Weaver, 17, a sister of the driver, had a broken rib and serious facial cuts.

"The other two passengers, Wayne Weaver, 18, and Joseph Hershberger, 18, suffered some cuts and bruises but no serious injuries. They were treated and released from the hospital.

"All were from Holmesburg except the victim, Anna Hostetler, and her cousin Sarah Hostetler who lived east of Breman.

"The state patrol says Weaver lost control of the vehicle on a slight curve. The youths were returning from a country music show in Wheeling, West Virginia, when the fatal mishap occurred. It is still not known whether charges will be filed against the driver Weaver.

"Anna Hostetler was the daughter of Mr. and Mrs. Melvin Hostetler of RD 5, Millersville. She was a member of the Old Order

Amish Church. Funeral services, planned for Tuesday, will be in charge of Samuel Troyer, bishop of the Doughty Valley District. The obituary appears on page 2."

They got the Jonas mixed up with Joseph, but the rest of it was about right. What they couldn't get was the pain in our minds and our hearts.

14.

Weep for me, O Israel. My face is in the water and I am sinking. Oh that I had a thousand eyes to shed my tears. That's what the psalmist said, I believe, or was it one of the prophets, maybe Jeremiah? Where is the goodness of God of which we talk and sing? Must we all go to our Father's home at the time he says so? Is there no consideration for our plans? Why did she have to die?

Ja, Gravey, preach. You are trying to show you're standing with me and having sympathy. Everybody pities me, but it makes nothing out. I do not need pity; I need what is right. I need my girl friend.

But pity was the only thing they could give to me and they did what they could. They all reached for my hand and said softly: "The Lord helps us," or *"Der Herr gibt und der Herr nimmt.* The Lord giveth and the Lord taketh." They squeezed my hand tightly and tried to make me feel it for sure. It was as if they knew that I was numb. *Ja*, they stood by me, but what was the point of it? I had to go down that lonely trail by myself.

Maybe Anna was better off, I thought. She is with God, and at least she didn't have to live with just the memory. Now I am a widower. But I knew it was just self-pity to think like this.

I looked over at Joseph the minister. He looked ten years older and sadder than an old owl. He had lost some sons to the world, and he knew what it was like. Chris sometimes carped at him for being a weakling, chewing tobacco and believing in works salvation, but even with all those troubles he had room to stand by me.

Gravey Ben kept on preaching the *Aanfang* at one of Anna's neighbors near Breman. "But we cannot understand the Lord's ways. The Lord is much greater than ourselves." He twisted his head. "I suppose Job many times had to ask, Why did God do these things?" He coughed. "But he remained faithful. And he kept on believing and doing what was right."

Gravey kept on jerking along in the same way that he always preached. He told the story of Job and the way that he had a lot of umph and push reminded me of how my life used to be. I looked at the boys down the row from me. A Sunday ago I was in their position, sitting there without any problems and thinking of the Cleveland Indians, our horses, and which girl was the nicest that I could get. There they sat, chewing hay stems and thinking of going swimming in the Hershberger pond tonight.

But I have lost my girl friend and my future wife. A week ago she had been living and twitching and alert and good. Today she is dead and gone. I am thinking of death and what might have been. O grave, you have the victory; o death, you have a sting.

"The apostle of the Patmos Island. He saw the vision of a new heaven and a new earth. It looked to him like a golden city. We could say that it was like a lush garden." Gravey kept on jerking his head, and the short sentences now came like regular beats, and I knew he was coming to the end.

"We can best understand the beautiful garden. The corn is 100 bushels to the acre. The flowers are of many colors. One could say it looks like the nice plots at the experiment station. But even that does not compare. We know that the Lord is great, and he will make it come out right." Gravey kept on talking about heaven, and I knew it was there, but it didn't help that much.

"But for the wicked, there is another place. Hell is as bad as heaven is good. Oh young ones, let us watch ourselves. Let us live our lives so that we will escape the fiery flames. These are prepared for the devil and his angels and not for God's people. Let us work. Let us hope. Let us be faithful."

I felt tired and looked down at the floor, then up to the barn doors where the coffin was sitting. I breathed and felt the air go and looked at my little nephews sitting on the other side of Chris and

making little pliers with hay stems. All they had to worry about
was their projects and going crazy, but now I couldn't help them. I
was in trouble with death.

"And if we are united," said Gravey, "let us pray." Everyone fell
on the floor and we prayed but I didn't know what to pray. I
couldn't pray to have her back. I couldn't pray to go with her. I
wasn't a Catholic so I couldn't pray for her in purgatory; God will
take care of her. My mind was as numb as my body.

As I looked out over that sea of black backs that were turned up to
the barn roof and to God, I thought of what *die Memm* used to tell us
when everything went bad and got dark. And it was getting dark
and hot outside. *Die Memm* said think of others. That's what she
said, think of others. So I tried to.

I thought of Toots and how he fought his wife with rods and
poles. I prayed for the neighbors. I prayed for Eisenhower our
president, that he would be smart and wise in leading our country.
I prayed for this Kennedy and vice-president Nixon who wanted to
be the next president, that whichever one won they would let the
Christians worship and live in peace and quietness. I prayed for the
communist Castro who had brought that godless religion to Cuba
and stirred up trouble. Then it all got blurry like the dead ducks in
Chris's driveway.

I don't think those prayers got any farther than the roof, and I
went numb again. And then I saw him. Roy was kneeling over near
the barn door with his big broad back up, praying to heaven with
the others. His ducktail was combed down in back, and he looked
down at the floor. There in a black suit and on his knees was my
brother who had a car and had brought us all to this grief. *Ja*, the
preachers will talk of heaven and hell, and he should hear it. Roy
had not been to an Amish church or worn our clothes for six years,
but there he was with the clothes which I found out later he had
borrowed from one of the Hershberger boys, and there was Jonas
beside him.

My feelings like my tears were so many that I didn't know which
were the strongest as I saw my prodigal brother. I didn't even know
if he had come home to stay, but I knew that I shouldn't think bad
thoughts of him if he is kneeling down and praying. I knew that I
didn't need to think bad of him because he was already suffering
enough. My neighbors had pity on me, but I don't think they had
any left for my brother.

It must have taken a lot for him to come because he knew it was
terrible and what he had done. At the same time, I knew that the

Hostetlers had talked to the state patrol and said they hoped no charges would be filed because everyone had suffered enough. Why do we have all this evil? I wasn't even angry when I saw Roy; I only felt cheated and sad.

"The Lord is great and greatly to be praised." It was Bishop Samuel Troyer, and now he was droning on. "And even on this sad occasion, we remember with the Psalmist of old and say, 'Bless the Lord . . .'" *Ja*, bishop you tried to comfort us and warned us for another hour, but I got more comfort from looking at Joseph, our own minister. He was sitting there with the rest of the ministers with his face like a scarecrow and his eyes tired and old.

Joseph looked down and seemed to be suffering for us all. You knew what trouble was, you old owl. Nobody spoke to me as comforting as you did when you came to me and said that there is purity in suffering. Is that what you have been feeling from the wildness of your boys, who have bought cars and have brought nothing but pain to your family? He had told me that if we accept our suffering we're like precious metal. We become better from heat and purifying. *Vell*, I didn't really understand that then, but he said it with so much conviction and feeling that it seemed true. It still seems strange to me that some of the main help and teaching I got during this time came from the worst farmer and weakest preacher in the district.

My eyes moved from Joseph to the other side of the barn and the women. There sat my older sisters and Martha with little Samuel, and they all had red eyes from crying. At the end of the row beside *die Memm* sat my bruised sister Leona, but her eyes were not wet and her head was not bent. If the rest had their heads bowed, Leona had her black and blue neck and jaw on display. Her body that pained with each step — what with her broken ribs — did not bring her to complain. She carried her sorrow as naturally as she did her shawl, and she seemed to be back to being the smartest person and the best friend I ever had.

If she went off balance with the *Englischer*, and by cracky she did, she was now back to herself again. She didn't pity me but she helped me. On the night before the funeral she told me to get out in the barn and help milk. "You don't think you can get out of the chores that easy, do you?" I wouldn't have had to because one of the neighbors came over, but it was good and it helped.

I looked out the open doors and the sky was dark to fit our spirits. The air was heavy and the sun had gone away. Outside I could see some of the *Buwe* going around to the buggies, closing the flaps and getting ready for the rain. Big drops began to plop on the tin roof, and Bishop Samuel Troyer's words were drowned in the water. Outside the open door I could see the fine dust spraying around when the first drops hit the dry earth.

I looked up and slumped further down into the bench. I felt tired and old and thought I would soon die like Anna. She had died of an auto crash. But I would die of sorrow and old age. The box still sat there with the rain crashing in from overhead. There would be no more rain walks, and the body in the coffin was still. I had looked for a long time that morning at the face that even in death had a slight smile, but the lip wouldn't move. For this life, it was all over.

By the time Sam Troyer finished, the rain slowed down, and we went to the graveyard. I stood by the hole listening to the sounds of the sticky wet little clods of earth hitting the rough box. The neighbors threw the shovels of dirt steadily, and it made sad music as first I heard the hollow thumpings from the coffin underneath and finally there was the muffled sound as the hole filled up. We are going down the hole one by one; human comfort in the hole we'll have none.

The hole was now about full and the pallbearers were tired. The only sound now was of the soft thud of pieces of earth meeting each other, the panting of the workers and the weeping of my family and friends. *Ja*, earth, take good care of her body, for God will take care of my *Meedel*. Heaven is waiting for her. She may not have been tame, but she was free like the birds and the butterflies; she was not bad. She followed the *Attnung*.

My mother and father stood on either side of me. *Die Memm* wept freely and dabbed her little white handkerchief to her eyes. She liked Anna and hoped she would make me a good wife. Ben was looking straight ahead, but a tear was lying at the bottom of his eyes. He held a stiff chin in his hand, but his head was bowed in submission. My feisty father who usually was a banty knew that we had no chance against death so he stood there and took it with his head down. But his muscles were strong, and I knew that tomorrow morning he would be crowing again.

Benny had me around the belly and held tightly. He didn't say anything but just squeezed me hard every now and then, and it helped me not to be so numb. Maybe he knew what I needed. I put my arm around his shoulders and held him. Then I noticed that he and Leona were about the only ones who didn't cry. They had other ways of standing with me. All around me were family and friends. *Ja*, Jeremiah. I do have a thousand eyes, and they are my friends who stand by me.

Across the hole were Anna's parents. Two weeks ago Anna and I snuck out of their living room, and Anna pinched me in the same way Benny was now squeezing me around the waist. We heard you Melvin and Clara, your breathing and your snoring. But now Melvin was crying freely, and Clara's eyes were red and her nose was runny. They had lost their daughter. I too am sad for you. You lost a good daughter who didn't deserve to die like this.

Across the hill was the orchard where we were that evening. Little did I think two weeks ago or on our Sunday afternoon walk that today I would be on the next knoll for the burial. Life and death — you are so close. She was my roamer one who always thought about leaving, but I'm sure she didn't think it would happen like this.

There are other Hostetlers in this yard and she will join them now in the peace which our Lord has prepared. Over at the side was one who was buried outside the graveyard. Poor man, to take his own life.

The earth was filled above the ground, and my eyes moved around the graveyard. That's where they met Roy's. He stood over in a corner all by himself like some rooster who had just been chased out of the flock. It was the first I noticed him out here. In the barn we all had to sit beside each other, but out here in the open air no one was with him. He looked so lonely and old and uncomfortable in his ducktail combed down and with that black suit on. His face was pale and with his scratches from the accident and everything, he looked like some old dark Cornish that had fought once too often.

I didn't even think twice what I did next because it was the only thing to do. I walked over to him and Benny went along. Roy didn't look up, and I knew he was sorry and that it had taken a lot for him to put on those clothes and come like this. Finally, he said, "*Ich wees yuscht gar net was zu saaga.* I just don't know what to say."

"*Es macht nix aus.* It doesn't matter," I said. "*Du brascht gar nix saaga.* You don't have to say a thing." We turned then and walked back to the Hostetlers' neighbors for the dinner.

15.

It was dusk. The air was cool, for the day had lost its warmth when the sun went down in the early evening. Flecha ran down the graveyard road toward Holmesburg, puffing and snorting into the evening and acting as if the load was as light as air. John was riding with me, and we were going to Chris and Martha's where he would leave me so I could catch the 5:10 bus early in the morning for Cleveland.

Flecha seemed to know this was the end of something and that she wouldn't give me too many rides like this. We were going to Holmesburg the way we had so many evenings when I went on dates, but now there was no one to go to.

We had two big suitcases crunched in with me in the buggy and a poke of food that *die Memm* sent along. My date was with Cleveland. It was the middle of September, and I was on my way to 1-W at the Cleveland City Hospital. It wasn't a hard decision to make because it was already made. I had lost my woman and I was drafted. I could have chosen a different hospital like Altman in Canton or something like that, but I had some friends at Cleveland so that seemed like the place to go.

And all at once I even wanted to go, even if I might not have wanted to admit it just like that. Everything at home reminded me of how my life had been and of Anna, and it even seemed to me that Joseph was right. I should be purified with some more suffering. I thought I was going through what the Coblentz widow went through when her young husband was killed over near Mt. Hope about five years ago.

Sometimes at night I'd half wake up and see Anna's dead body with the pink scarf on the head lying dead on the ground where I found her that night. Then I'd see Paul Coblentz lying in his own doorway, shot by two drunken soldiers who had no business being even near there. Then I'd see his widow — she looked just like Anna — crying, and I wanted to cry with her. I knew it was just self-pity to think that I was one of the Coblentzes and that I shouldn't think this way.

At Holmesburg Flecha clip-clopped down through the main street, and I stopped in at Wengert's Supermarket and picked up some Snickers. We just stopped along the street, and I told John to hold on to Flecha while I picked up the Snickers.

But then LaMar Wengert got ahold of me at the counter, and he all at once took a special interest in me.

"I hear you're going to Cleveland."

"Yup," I said. "1-W."

"That's a tremendous opportunity to witness."

"Huh."

"*Ja*, here so many people have heard so often. But there you'll see so many people who are down and out." His eyes turned toward the ceiling, and I could tell he really wished he were up there in Cleveland witnessing. "*Ja*, here you have to be careful that you don't offend anyone. See, I have to because these people are my customers. But there at the hospital, what a natural place to witness and bring them to Christ."

"I hadn't thought of it like that," I said.

"Well, you should," he said. "Too many of these *Buwe* just go up there for two years and help the sick, make friends and do their work and all that, but they don't take advantage of the tremendous opportunity to witness."

I think he was really sincere, but then Gravey Ben, our bishop, came in and he changed his tune just like that. Poor LaMar. Gravey was one of his customers. "God bless you, Wayne," he said, as I paid for the Snickers and left.

At Chris's the three boys along with a few town boys were playing rabbit in the front yard. It was school time again, and everyone was playing rabbit. We used to play it when I was in school, and it was one of those games that stuck like softball, volleyball and basketball.

"Come on, help us," they all said in one voice. They came panting up to us at the tree where we hitched Flecha. "*Ja*, John," I said. "Why don't we help them play for a while?"

"Makes me nothing out," said John and so we played rabbit. I probably shouldn't have done it, what with being almost 19 years old and all, but every now and then you do things like that that are good, even if they aren't your age.

It was a hunting game and one was it, and he would count to 20 while the rest would leave base. Then the hunter would go look for the rest — I'm not sure what we were, rabbits, I guess, or horses or wolves — and everybody tried to get back without getting hit by the hunter's ball. If you got hit, then you were a dog and you had to help catch the others, holding them till the hunter came with the ball.

At first some of the small and fast ones could get away by dodging the ball. After there were several dogs a lot of it was muscles, and so John and I were usually the last ones caught. It was most often John because he was strong as a bull and fast too. I said that we were rabbits, but most of the time we ran like horses or wolves out in the West. When we'd take off from base we'd snort and gallop and whinny and trumpet like mustangs out on the Great Plains.

We all thought we were the black stallion in Walter Farley's books about the horse which couldn't be tamed by a rope. We were the fine Arabian which won every race out on the desert. At other times we were the timber wolf which got away from guns and deadly bait and stayed wild and howling out on the prairie. Judas, it was fun and John put on quite a show for his little nephews, and the town boys who called him Lobo. He galloped the highest and trumpeted so loud, I thought he was going to split his pants. Everybody laughed and it was a disgrace, but it didn't matter because we were all just boys.

On the last round we played, everyone was caught but John, and he broke through the tackles of the boys two times and came home. Finally, on the third time, I got my hands on him, and we pulled him down like a pack of wolves on a buffalo. I was at the bottom of the pile with six little boys on top and John kicking like a bull when I heard the gravel crackle in the driveway. Matthew was it, and he came and tapped John with the ball, and slowly the pile came apart.

Then I saw who was in the drive.

Sitting parked along the drive were our ministers Gravey Ben Miller and Joseph Yoder, both hanging their heads out the side and with their big eyes watching us. Judas, this was some way to meet my ministers the last night before I go off to 1-W, but there they were. It was getting dark, but I thought they were even smiling a little. Anyway, it took care of our game, and the town boys turned for the road to Holmesburg. Before they went, they begged Lobo and me to come back another evening.

I didn't go into where I was going, but my little lobo brother kind of hitched himself up and changed right into a man again. He said *vell* he'd have to be getting on home, and even though he couldn't come back and play rabbit every evening, he could give them a ride back to town, if they wanted. Boy, did that give them a jerk, and they raced for the buggy.

John then turned to me and there in his grass stained and rumpled clothes that were all scratched, I had never seen a bigger 16-year-old in my life. We just stood there for a little, and I took his hand. "Take good care of *die Memm* and Dad," I said, and "Write me sometimes."

"Yup," he said and I knew he would take good care of my parents and would not write. He just stood some more, and I don't think either of us had done farewells like this before. If there was something you were supposed to say, neither one of us knew the line.

"Don't let'em change you too much," he said, and then the town boys who had piled in the buggy yelled, "Hey Lobo, let's go!"

John turned and walked over to the buggy and told those little *Englischer* that, by cracky, if they didn't sit down and be quiet right now, they'd be walking to town as fast as you can say "Rabbit." He took the reins and as I watched him take my horse, I knew that my little brother was growing up. Even his last words were the same as my father Ben had given me several hours ago in the kitchen: "Don't let'em change you too much."

What a line. I never forgot it even when I later made plenty of changes in Cleveland. Maybe that's what you were supposed to say at these farewells. Anyway, both my old man and my little brother said it, and I knew it came from their hearts. The town boys waved to my little nephews, Flecha snorted, the ducks hissed and squawked and then they were gone.

I gave the boys their Snickers, and they were crunching away as we went over to the ministers' buggy. Joseph was looking out the side, looking lonelier than an old crow with his tired horse. We must have looked like the dickens, what with our scratched and dirty clothes from playing rabbit.

Gravey Ben sat on the other side, and I knew now why I had seen him at Wengert's Supermarket. They had met there and come over here for a visit with Chris. One look at Gravey's face and I knew that something was wrong, and he was going to make it right. It probably had something to do with the *Attnung*, and the way Gravey sat with his hard face, sitting there stiff as a board, let me know that Chris was in trouble. No-sir-ee, they didn't come just to say goodbye to me.

God must have known what he was doing when he had the lot fall on Gravey Ben because he really knew how to hold the line. Joseph didn't even know how to hold the line with his own boys, and everyone knew that if he ran the church the way he did his farm, the line fences would soon have too many holes in them. He always looked tired and as if he carried all our pains on his weak shoulders. Still, we loved him and when we had problems, we often went to Joseph. Gravey was right, but Joseph was loved.

"You'll not do too much of this up in Cleveland," said Gravey.

"Naw, guess not."

"How's the duck business?" he asked my nephews.

"We do okay as long as Dad doesn't charge us too much for feed," said Matthew. The other boys were still chewing Snickers and panting and laughing. I knew well enough that they didn't pay anything for the feed.

"Is your Dad here?"

"*Ja*, he's in the house."

"Could we see him a little?"

"*Ja*, come on in," said Aden.

"Naw, we'll wait out here."

"*Ja*, we'll get him," said Aden, and he galloped off to the house. And I knew he would find an unhappy father. The ministers wanted to talk about the *Attnung* or other church affairs, and I knew that Chris didn't believe in it the way they did. One evening after the funeral Chris told me about what he called his "enlightenment," which changed the way he looked at things. He said he now understood the truth and that Gravey Ben and Joseph Yoder were deeply stuck in tradition, and it's dead stuff.

"Tradition is nothing," he said. "Salvation is only in the gift of God by the blood of Christ, and you can know it when you have it." I knew he was getting these ideas from the Moody books LaMar

Wengert was peddling to him. Anyway, it really gave him a new spirit and life.

He spent long evenings translating English tracts into German and German history things into English. He wrote articles and read all about our beginnings with the Anabaptists and the Reformation. "It's so simple," he said. "All are lost in sin, but through faith in Christ we can be saved and walk in the newness of life. And if we are saved, we can know it."

Chris acted as though it was the biggest surprise in his life that he had lived for 35 years and didn't know this simple truth. Chris used to tell me that all we needed was moral teaching and education. Now he added a third thing we needed: assurance of salvation. He looked me right in the eyes and said: "You can't just live on hope; you have to know it."

The evening he gave this lecture to me, I wasn't in a mood to argue with him because I didn't really know what all it meant. It was something against the ministers and the church, I thought, and it had to do with things like hope and assurance of salvation, but I didn't see that the one was better than the other.

I think we looked at it like he was always interested in new ideas — like the time he found out that the key to good health was radiant heat. Radiant heat was when he closed all the cold air registers in the house after the Yoders had put in a new furnace in the basement. Or another time he discovered that the key to good health was the purest food, the grape. So he went on a grape diet for several weeks.

As near as I could see, his assurance of salvation was just another grape diet or radiant heat. And I knew that as long as he didn't stir up the people, was good to his sons and kept to his farming and the *Attnung*, no one cared that much whether he had hope or assurance.

But now I was worried about Chris, and I knew that Martha would get after his ideas if they made problems in the church. Had he done something silly like the time he sang a second part during the *Lob Lied*? Had he called the ministers Pharisees or done something terrible like that?

Chris walked out to us and greeted us.

"Good evening," Gravey said. "Gets dark so early already."

"You can step down and come on in."

"Naw, this is fine," said Joseph.

It was quiet for a little and Joseph's tired little brown mare would just every now and then stomp her feet down hard. The little boys kept chewing but had sense enough not to say anything.

"*Vell,* have you started shocking corn too?" asked Gravey, breaking the silence.

"No, we're still cutting," said Chris. But I knew what he was thinking. Why are my people always talking about farming? There are important spiritual things to talk about and all my people want to talk about is farming. Do you have the wheat shocked? Did you get the pigs weaned?

"*Vell,* I'm in the same situation," Joseph said. He carefully wrapped the reins of the little horse around the post of the buggy as if he was going to stay for a while.

"Our problem," said Gravey Ben, "is to know what to do with the corn. The price that hogs are now, we might as well sell it instead of feeding it."

Joseph: "You can never tell, they usually go up again around Christmas time."

"*Vell,* last week at Kidron they were still way down," said Gravey. "Twelve cents a pound. You can't feed hogs for that price."

"Naw, that's right, It's at this time when it's good to be diversified," Joseph said that last word in English. "I've discussed this with McMillen. He says the strong part of our way of life is diversified farming. That way if the hogs aren't good, we have the milk or the eggs or wheat."

"*Ja,* sure, we've always done it like that," said Gravey.

McMillin was the county agent and was usually full of hot air, but we knew he was right about being diversified. "It's kinda something the way what is actually nicer and better for us is also more economical," I said. "You can soon lose your shirt in specialized farming."

"You can easily depend too much on one thing. We've seen that from the broiler business and the way some are even now trying to specialize in hogs," said Joseph. He looked at Chris and his three boys who hadn't said a word yet in all of this. "Your family is not too diversified yet, is it?"

"*Ja,* you're going to have a good bunch of helpers in the fields one of these days," said Gravey.

"*Ja,* I have already," said Chris. "They have given me a lot of help in whatever I'm doing. But they get in the road some too." I knew that Chris wanted to sound humble to the ministers, but he was almost proud of his sons and often said so to me.

"Children are a great blessing from the Lord," said Joseph in a tone like he was going into a sermon. "One could say that they are the Eternal's hope for the future. Soon we'll be using canes and needing help and then another generation will be ready to step in." He spit a chew of tobacco out on the ground and held his head like he had a deep spiritual thought, but I knew that wasn't Chris's idea of a spiritual thought.

"And they always come. Isn't it something that there is always a group of the faithful? Some lose the way, but they always come. It's a blessing." His slow voice and sad owl eyes turned to amazement and wonder when he looked at my little nephews.

"*Ja*, but sometimes I wonder if we don't have more wild and *litterlich* ones today," said Gravey. "We've just never had the temptations for our young people like the ones we have today. Look what it brings us to." He looked over at me, and I knew he was thinking of Wheeling and funerals and all that. "Sometimes it looks dark."

"Moral teaching," said Chris. "That's what we need more of. Our young people need teaching of what the Scriptures say about what's right and wrong."

"*Vell*, I must always marvel at the goodness of God that he has given another generation of boys and girls who we feed and care for and teach in godly ways. They grow up and learn our way, marry one of our people, settle down with time and carry on the Christian faith." Joseph looked over at me. "And even if they go to 1-W, we know they'll come out all right. *Nee, mir setta net zu engschtlich vata.* No, we shouldn't become too anxious. The Lord is our refuge and will care for his people. We simply need to be faithful, stay together and keep the unity of the church. It's very important for the next generation to learn that." Joseph looked Chris right in the eyes: "*Ja*, Chris, you are truly many times blessed."

Joseph kept on going like this, and I think I remembered it because it was the last evening I was at home. My little nephews weren't that interested though, and they were squirming around. Anyway, all of us older ones knew that why the ministers came was to see Chris.

"Aden, go close the brooder house door and see that all the chickens are inside," said Chris. "And Matthew and Raymond, go along and help."

"Let's go." Aden grabbed Raymond's arm and the boys galloped off together, slapping each other on the back like cowboys out on the plain.

Two minutes later they were back. "Did you check that every broiler was inside?" asked Chris.

"*Ja*," they answered together and out of breath.

"How about your projects? Are they all fed?"

"*Ja*."

"Then go see that the hogs have some fresh water yet this evening."

"We did that already," Raymond said.

"Go do it again," said Chris, now getting a little mad.

The ministers got back on the fall corn crop and seeding some wheat, but then the boys were right back. This time Chris sent them in to Martha.

"Go in to the house and check the wood supply." The little boys looked at their father as if he had just slipped two notches, and I'm sure they were thinking that's how Daniel got to Massilon too. But they didn't say anything in front of the ministers. Inside the house Martha caught them, and we were by ourselves.

Gravey Ben soon started in: "Somebody put it to us that you have a little rubber wheeled pony cart with balloon tires."

I squinted my eyes to look over under the maple tree where the cart had been sitting. Chris pointed over in the same direction. "*Ja*, the boys have one that's sitting over there. I wanted to give them some kind of a pony cart to ride around in." Chris looked down and looked sad.

"*Vell*," said Joseph, "it's getting to be time for communion and some of these things should be taken care of."

"*Ja*, I simply didn't know it was a problem. I would have thought because there are no tubes in it and no air pumped in . . ."

"We don't want to be critical, and we all have our faults, but we just wanted to mention this because some people have mentioned it to us."

"*Ja vell*, some people, of course, wouldn't know that we don't have any tubes in it," said Chris.

There was a pause.

"Then we were wondering . . . we know that you have lived here several years now, and we're wondering if it isn't time that electric water pump be changed over to a gasoline engine." Gravey Ben put it nice but you could tell he meant business and, Judas, it was way too long for Chris to not have shut off the electric.

Chris looked down, "*Ja*, I've just let that go too long." His voice cracked and we could tell that he really did know he was in hot water. I also knew of a little light bulb back in the cattle shed. Maybe the ministers knew of this too.

"I'll see to it that it's changed in the next week. We've simply had so much work. I've let some of these things slide for too long."

"We don't want to be critical and we all have our faults," Joseph said in his sad voice. "But we must mention these things to you as a brother. We're all concerned about keeping the unity with the *Attnung* and the church, to keep it pure and holy."

"*Ja* sure, these are some things I've just been careless about and anyway I have a Briggs and Stratton in the shed; it's just a matter of changing it over." I think he was really sorry, and all at once assurance of salvation, moral teaching and all those other fancy words he'd talked about seemed as far away as the man in the moon.

No one said anything for a while and then Chris said, "Do you think the boys' little cart is a problem if people know it doesn't have any inflated tubes?"

Gravey coughed nervously. I knew he didn't want to give in on anything.

Finally Joseph said slowly, "*Ja*, I'm glad to know that now, and it's some different. But we do want to stay together on this one. See, if we get inflated rubber tires it will be just another step to the car and the tractor, and we can't have them. Our way of living depends on seeing each other, visiting, helping each other and staying close to the home farm and community. When people get cars they run all over the place."

"*Ja*, I used to work for Grassbaugh and all his tractors and you get a lot done. But they had no tranquility. That family was running all over the place with cars and tractors and motorcycles and what have you," said Gravey. "Still, at the end of the year they had less money left over than we do."

Chris didn't say anymore and then we started talking some more of Gravey Ben's son who had been kicked by a horse. The ministers wished me well and a safe trip up to Cleveland and told me to come back when I could. Gravey gave me a strong handshake and Joseph winked at me with his old owl eyes and said, "Don't let those *Englischer* change you too much." Judas, what a line. Even Chris gave it to me the next morning at the bus.

Then the little brown mare was heading down the driveway, and Chris took me over to the shed and showed me the little Briggs and Stratton. I think he wanted to let me know before I left that he did want to follow the *Attnung* and keep the unity of the church. *Die Memm* wrote me a few weeks later that he confessed in church that it had taken him way too long to change over to the gasoline motor and that he wanted to keep the unity of the brotherhood. Both he and Martha took communion then.

When we got in the house the little boys wanted to know what our visit was all about, and Chris said that we were just getting things straightened out for the fall harvest, and they'd better get to bed if they wanted to see me off in the morning. We took the lantern then and headed up the stairs.

"It was the electric pump, wasn't it?" said Aden as soon as we got to the top of the stairs. "*Ja,*" I said, "it's high time to get that little Briggs and Stratton on there." But I didn't tell them about the pony cart.

16.

The days became shorter and the sun came up late. Exactly when the sun came out, I'm not sure because for the first time in my life I was sleeping late in the morning. I worked at Cleveland City Hospital from three to 11 and would open my eyes to see the sun at nine in the morning, at least when the smog was not too strong and the clouds would let it shine. Smog, *ja*, it was a new word for me. Usually I could see the sun when it came above the top of the tall warehouse which was to the east of my apartment building. That was my new home for two years.

I had been in Cleveland about a month. And I actually liked it there and working in the hospital and all. It's one of those things I can't explain, that Anna, who had wanted to get out of our life and meet the world never would, and I, who had never really wanted to, now did.

But life is like that. We can't control it and it plays tricks on us. We are just checkers on a board we never chose to get on. We get moved from one spot to another by some hand we can't control, and we don't even know the rules of the game. Sometimes we're jumped and taken out of the game. Sometimes we're kings. And now I've been jumped, and I'll suffer just because I was sitting on a certain space.

Those kind of thoughts didn't stay too long though because

there was also a lot of good. I walked over to the window and looked out at the sun that was now shining softly through the smog. A flock of pigeons flew past the building, and I heard their fluttering swoosh. I went to the bathroom and peed and looked carefully if it was light or dark. Ah, it was light and I was healthy and feeling well.

I went back to the window and watched the cars and the people in the street below going who knows where. Yup, this life in the city is treating me much better than I ever expected. I should have suffered more like the soldiers when they go to boot camp and training. But here I am getting up late in the mornings, seeing the sun shine through the clouds, listening to a flock of pigeons swoosh by and peeing in light colors. Not bad.

That's what I thought as I went back to the bathroom and shaved. I was trying to grow a full beard, but it was a mixture of peach fuzz and bare spots and a few long hair that didn't belong anywhere. But I shaved my upper lip and my neck anyway, and then I sat down on the beat-up couch and read a chapter from the Psalms. Joseph had sent me a German-English New Testament, and it also had the Psalms and Proverbs and I read from them in the mornings.

Wohl dem, der sich des Dürftigen annimmt!
Den wird der Herr erretten zur bösen Zeit.
Der Herr wird ihn bewahren und beim Leben erhalten
und es ihm lassen wohl gehen auf Erden
und wird ihn nicht geben in seiner Feinde willen.

Blessed is he who considers the poor!
The Lord delivers him in the day of trouble;
the Lord protects him and keeps him alive;
he is called blessed in the land;
thou dost not give him up to the will of his enemies.

I kept on reading and knew just how blessed I was when I looked at the other people around. Some were poor and slept in the street. Others were rich and looked like a million dollars. They must have had some too. Someone had to pay for all those buildings. I thought of Sandy, my nurse friend at the hospital, and I thought of my brother Roy in some barracks, who knows where.

I thought of the drunks and winos we dried out at the hospital every night and the whores who wandered the streets on the weekends.

Could they look forward to a life in the open fields and having a loyal dog and a faithful high-stepping horse? Did they have a mom and a dad who helped them get established and off on the right foot? Judas, I bet some of them didn't even know who their parents were. Did they have a humble minister like Joseph and a strict young bishop like Gravey who gave you good rules and stood with you when you were in trouble? Did they have a brother like John who all at once grew up and you liked him like your right arm or little nephews like the little Yoders? I looked at those people, and then I was glad Leona just liked hillbilly music.

Ja, I must be thankful. The day is good; God has made the earth and we live on it.

I went to the table and picked up Wyman's clothes. *Kosslich*, sloppy, why doesn't he put his things away? He always leaves everything lying around like some *lumpa nest*. But I liked living with Wyman who was from the Maple Valley District west of Millersville.

Wyman Mast had been in Cleveland for over a year and knew everything about living in this place so he was handy to have around. He worked at Cleveland City during the day, and at night he went to see the Indians. "I won't live in Cleveland forever," he would say. "I'll have to watch them lose while I have the chance."

There were about a dozen of us from Holmes County up here in 1-W so you could stay up on what was going on around home, and there was always enough travel back and forth that we kept well supplied with Trail balogna and Swiss cheese.

I heated water for coffee so I could make coffee soup for breakfast and then went to the refrigerator for some cheese and a piece of *muschmelon*. *Ja*, I know the English is muskmelon or cantaloupe, but I say *muschmelon* sometimes, just to make a point. One time we bought some from a young squirt at a roadside stand and Leona asked for *muschmelons*. He made such a big thing over the way she said *musch* that I'd still like to plaster that *muschmelon* right in his face, if I wouldn't be nonresistant. You always have a few *Englischer* smart alecks and some ex-Amish who make us out to be dumb hicks. *Vell*, maybe we don't always speak the king's English, but I've heard enough different kinds of English here in Cleveland to know that the king must have a lot of different speakers out there. Anyway, that fellow should have had more respect for my sister.

After breakfast I went down the seven flights of wooden stairs on the outside. I could also go down the inside, but the morning was so nice and I wanted to get as much of the fresh air as I could. I lit a cigar and puffed little clouds up into the fresh air. It was a quiet day because not many people were out on the street early on Sunday morning. Just off and on a car and the busses were running. I headed for the newsstand to get the Sunday paper.

I had the time to read. For the first time in my life I had so much time on my hands it seemed like eternity. We only worked for eight hours a day and then had two days off on weekends so I read. I read the scriptures like I did this morning. I found new things in the Bible that lifted me up and helped me answer some questions, not only mine but those of people I met.

Judas, I never answered so many questions in my life. My life was one big question mark for the *Englischer*. They sure had a lot. Sometimes I felt like just doubling over and putting a dot under me for the questions that I was. Why do you wear a beard? Why don't you believe in going into the army? Why this? Why that? *Vell*, why not? I say. Why do you only work eight hours in a day? Why do you have to lock everything? Why don't people trust each other?

But I was reading. I read the *Plain Dealer* every day to get the news. I read it like a drunk who needed his wine, page after page, column after column, line by line, right down to the little letters that bunched together to say things to me. I read the news pages, the Dear Abby advice (I didn't agree with her half the time), Action Line and an article on skiing. I read about Nikita Khrushchev coming to New York, talking to the United Nations and pounding his shoe on the table. They said he used to be a potato farmer.

I really got interested in the elections and watched for each move of Nixon and Kennedy. I looked carefully at the photos of Nixon, the second stringer on the Whittier College football team and the second stringer on Eisenhower's president team. What was a Quaker doing playing football and running for president? I couldn't imagine Malcolm doing a thing like that. I hoped Kennedy would lose because he was Catholic and who knows what he and the Pope might try to do. But I liked him for his family and the way they were a big tribe. "A good family," I told Wyman when I looked at the big Kennedy family picture in the paper with the old grandmam and the grandchildren all on it. "They'll do all right because they stick together."

But more than anything I liked the sports page. I read of the Olympics in Rome in September, and, boy, did I stay up on the Yankees. *Ja*, I know I liked Cleveland like I like little children and women, but I had to respect those Yankees like a big strong uncle. I memorized all the batting averages without trying to, and I'd feel bad when Mickey's average would drop a point. I felt good all day when Roger Maris or Elston Howard hit another home run.

The Yankees played the Pirates in the first game of the World Series, and I had listened to most of it on the little transistor radio Wyman had. Now today I wanted to read it again in the paper. These things got better every time you went over them. Five blocks down on Euclid Avenue was the newsstand, and you could have missed it for the litter.

"Why can't they keep this place clean?" I said as I kicked a beer can and then picked it up. "Beer cans, newspapers, pee and candy wrappers all over the place."

Still I liked Cleveland. During the week I liked the busyness, the work, and the noise and the many people. There on the street you met so many different people you could have written a book about them. Business people with little thin leather carrying bags, women all covered with fur, little children going to school.

For the first time in my life I saw a lot of Negroes. They were black and brown and tan and red and all kinds of tones, but I saw them everywhere. I saw them on the street, at the hospital and in the stores. I laughed when I remembered the little pygmies from Malaysia we studied in geography in school. *Vell*, Africans in Cleveland were not little pygmies; this was big and tall Africa with big lips and big butts. Judas, the way things get turned around. I had always considered Negroes strange, and here they seemed natural. I was the strange one.

I think I liked Cleveland too because it kept my mind off of Anna. The people, the traffic, the noise and the new way of living kept my mind busy on other things. I began to feel that I was a part of this larger group but still totally different. I knew I couldn't do much here in this confusion and that I wasn't very important. Nobody even knew me. But while I was here I'd take care of the sick, the cripples and the drunks at City Hospital.

A dog came trotting down the street looking important. He had a blocky head and short hair like Bounce, but he had one white eye. I whistled to him, but he paid no attention to me. "Come on, who are you and where are you going?" I actually said it out loud to him, but he kept on trotting down Euclid.

And who are you to ask me that kind of question? he seemed to say to me. *Vell* that's what I thought.

"I'm Wayne Weaver from Holmes County. That's who I am." I said it out loud again and I laughed. I felt so terribly alone that even a dog wouldn't pay any attention to me, and at the same time I felt a part of everything. I turned my head and watched the terrier. "Ben's Wayne, that's who I am. Lost my woman, that's what I did." I could say this out loud right there on the street same as I used to talk to myself when I'd ride the mower and everything was rattling like a freight train. Only here someone might actually hear me but it didn't matter. By cracky, this place is used to crazy people. This city is full of people who are off their rockers, and that's why I like it here and feel a part of everything.

It was strange because here I was an outsider, and I noticed everything. Things that others took for granted, I got very interested in, I guess in about the same way some people were interested in me. You noticed things you hadn't seen before. It helped me to see how my life in Holmes County had never seemed special to me, and how it must have been strange to some people. Still, here I felt part of everything because everyone was an outsider.

The dog turned the corner at Euclid, and I didn't see him any more. Never met him again. Where was he going? Who did he belong to? Where did all the dogs and all the men and women who stood along the street get their money, their food and their jobs? Were they on welfare? What did they all do in those offices? Where did they sleep? Were they like the dogs in the country who slept under logs and in the wild? But here there were no logs. I got all my people and animals mixed up together here, but the lines weren't very clear to me here in the city.

I went back to the apartment and climbed the seven stairways. They creaked as I lightly jumped on each one like a cat. At the top I stopped and dug into my pockets for the keys.

The key. *Da Schlissel.* Never had I used so many keys. Everything needed a key. Everything was locked at the hospital from drawers to windows. My apartment had three locks, but I used only two of them, plus the chain lock which was fastened on the inside. At night the stores were locked and barred and some even had fences in front of the windows. Judas, Cleveland spent half its time locking and unlocking. Even the police locked their horses when they left them along the street. One evening out at the Ball Stadium there were some police on horses, and I checked on a horse tied to some chicken fence behind the stadium. Sure enough, there was a little padlock on the horse's rein. No wonder the mayor gave a key to important visitors to the city.

I made some popcorn to eat before I got started in on the paper. That was our Sunday afternoon and evening food, but since today I'd be at the hospital at that time it also tasted good in the morning.

I sat down on the dilapidated couch and looked for the sports section. There was the same story I heard on the radio the day before. The Pirates had won the first game of the World Series, 6–4, and it was the good pitching of the Mormon Vernon Law and a relief pitcher called Elroy Face who did it.

Good pitcher, that Law. But wait till those Yankee bats start banging, and then it'll be another story.

I went back to the front page. There was a picture of Nixon, Eisenhower and Henry Cabot Lodge waving their hands at a meeting at New York's Madison Square Garden. Big crowd. You'd think this politics was really important. Kennedy was getting ready to make a half-hour TV show with his Vice President, Lyndon Johnson of Texas. I'd never heard much of this Johnson before. The poll takers said that the election was too close to call.

Sometimes I thought maybe we should vote so the Catholics wouldn't win, but deep down I knew that Bush Mike's Mart was right. We didn't have to take sides on that president. Let the Catholics and Protestants fight it out however they wanted to. If they wanted to fight a war or if they came to get our horses, they might be Catholics or Protestants or any other religion, for all we knew.

Then there was another picture of Castro. I was always interested in his picture because he looked like some Amishman who had joined the Holdermans and stopped shaving his mustache. Castro said that he wasn't taking sides on the American elections because neither of the two candidates were able to tell the truth. "Both," he said, "are two beardless kids, puppets who are toys of the great interests." *Vell*, he was a terrible communist and communists were liars, but he said some truth too.

I kept on going through the pages and then got to the Sunday magazine inside the paper. On the cover was a familiar face with an army cap on the head and a title that said, "A Long Way from the Fields." It was Roy. I felt bad and at first didn't want to read it but I had to. I knew it would say things that shouldn't be said. That's the way these writings always are when they're written for the public. They say private things that should only be talked about at home, but people like to read about these things. So they're printed to sell papers.

The article was supposed to be about the Amish, but it was mainly about Roy and when he left and why he joined the Army and now the Air Force. It was just the way they always did it. Someone who has left us tells the story of who we are and all that.

And it's always a bad picture because that's why they left.

I read through the article and looked at the picture of Roy when he was in the sixth grade and had long straight hair and suspenders. Roy told the reporter of life on our farm and how he grew up. He said that he liked the land and the soil and that if he would ever amount to anything it was because he used to rub his feet around in the plow furrows. He didn't mention that he hated the animals and had never liked to farm for as long as I can remember.

He said that the Amish religion was doomed because it was too far behind the times and couldn't change. He told how backward the Amish were because they don't go to school more than the eighth grade, don't use electricity and don't use deodorant. "It's too bad they are not educated," he said.

"They say one thing but then they do something else," he said. "That's what got to me. They do not own cars or telephones, but then they use them if they belong to other people." Judas, he should know better than that.

"They are so legalistic that a person cannot be himself. What if you want to be an individual and different from the others? No-sir-ee, the bishops and the old men who control the money won't allow that. They don't want you to be an individual; they just want you to be like them, like the group. I saw through that."

I hope he doesn't say anything too bad about *die Memm* and Dad, I thought. Some day he'll regret it. I thought he might use the article to get even with Ben, but he didn't mention our father.

Vell, it wasn't only the bad part of us, at least as he saw it. He also told of his problems with the world since he left us. He told of his problems with the law, his problems with his wife and with the way other people thought and did things. I didn't even know that he had a wife. He never told us that. But Roy said how that he and his wife were raised different and how they thought different about things.

I was glad I read the piece because it gave me a side of Roy that I didn't know of before. He had his troubles too out in the world, and it sounded like he and his wife had problems too. It helped me to look at him from his side. Maybe he wasn't trying to be bad. I must be more like Christ and love him just as he is. But most of all I could never forget the last statement that he made. This was the way it ended: "The only thing I ever did in my life that I'm proud of was to break away from the Amish because it took a lot of courage. But I'd never recommend it to anyone else because I couldn't tell them where to go."

17.

At two o'clock I slipped into my white hospital clothes. After a month, they still felt strange on me. It was one of the hardest things for me to get used to wearing those white pants with a zipper and belt. For the first few days I felt guilty and felt as if everybody was looking at me, maybe even Gravey Ben, our bishop. I can see why one of the Swartzentrubers wouldn't do it to wear a uniform, period.

But our minister Joseph Yoder had told us it was all right to wear them at the hospital, if those were the regulations. He just didn't want us to bring them home. I really knew that nobody in the city cared what kind of clothes I put on; I could be English or Amish whichever I wanted to be. *Vell*, it wasn't quite like that, but that's the way it seemed with the clothes.

At the bus stop I watched the faces. It was my hobby, looking at the faces, and I was the only one who did it. Nobody looked you in the eyes, and you would have thought it was against the rules. Judas, I'd never seen so many different faces before, and I thought sometime I'd see one I'd know. But I never did. They must have known they wouldn't see a friend here so they didn't even try. They were dark and light, wrinkled and smooth, scarred and bright with make-up. The eyes would look at me and then go down or off to the side or straight ahead. That was it—straight ahead.

People could look right straight ahead and still not look at you.

I got on the bus, and at the next stop we picked up a huge woman. What a load of hay. She got onto the first step and just stood there panting and puffing. Her glasses were fogged shut, but I could see down at her eyes from above where I was sitting. She stared straight ahead and mumbled something to nobody. At the next stop some more people got on and they just squeezed past her at the door step. Nobody told her to move, and she just stood there like a big barn post in the middle of the aisle.

She grunted and took another step up and got to the top. She panted some more, and then put the money in the counter box. Her head went down as she looked over the top of her glasses and spotted me and the empty seat beside me. Slowly, one step at a time and panting all the way, she came. I would have taken her bags, but I tried that once and the person cracked me one. I guess she thought I was trying to steal them.

I looked around and no one else was paying any attention to this woman, but I watched her closely. She plopped down in the seat and I expected to see the dust rise the way it did when we dropped a load from the grapple hooks. Slowly she took off her glasses and cleaned them.

Why was she so tired? Where was she going? Why was she colored? Why was she so heavy? I knew I shouldn't ask, and they weren't questions I could put to anyone. I looked around on the bus. Two little boys were giggling and pinching each other several seats back. Behind me were two old men, talking about something really important the way they looked, ignoring everyone else. You'd look at them, and you would have thought they were the only ones in the bus. Otherwise, no one was talking; everyone was reading a newspaper or a book or looking straight ahead. Yup, that was the favorite. Looking straight ahead. A young girl held a transistor radio to her ear.

Who were they and did they care who I was? Did they know that on cool mornings in the fall, I had stood with my bare feet in the warm spots where horses were lying overnight? This Negro beside me, still panting. She must have had bad lungs. She would have had a story too behind those foggy glasses and dark eyes. Was her grandfather a slave? Did she have children? A husband? She looked at me then and said, "Hello." I must have been staring at her because I about didn't say anything back to her, but I smiled.

It felt so good to smile because she said hello to me, and I knew no one cared if I smiled anyway. If the little boys back there could giggle, I could smile when I felt good. I forgot all those questions and just thought of that friendly woman beside me and then before we could say much more we were at the bus stop, and I had to get off. "I'm getting off here," I said. And she said the nicest thing: "Now you have a good day, boy."

It was the kind of thing *die Memm* or my sister Martha would have said, and I was still smiling from it when I met Sandy Green in the hall at City Hospital. She looked at me kind of funny because she knew that I liked her and I think she enjoyed it. We often worked together on the tenth floor, and I probably got to know her better that first month than I did anyone else in Cleveland. I liked her, but I think it was too much the physical.

She was a little black Sarah: neat and fit and a perfect body. Her two black eyes were alert and lively, and her nose was small and pointed but seemed to fit right on her face. When she laughed — and she often did — a little dimple would come to her cheek. And she had two little breasts that pointed right at you, and that I thought of way too much.

She reminded me a little of a black pacer: small, sensitive, a little skittish, but still good.

"Just in time, Weaver." That's what she always called me. "We've got a bad one tonight."

"*Ja,* what?"

"Big accident at the University. A music concert. Can you imagine, of all the places to have an accident. They're down in the emergency room getting sewed together."

"I'll be bringing them up after a while, uh?"

"Yes, those who make it."

I went down the hall and thought of her two little breasts. They had a life of their own, just like the Bible saw them as two fawns, twins of a gazelle, that feed among the lilies. I even read the Ecclesiastes poem again and saw that the two lovers were of different races and thought this fit us alright. But I knew I shouldn't think about the physical too much. I tried to forget her as I went from room to room checking temperatures, giving cold water and changing bed pans.

And then I got into Phil Cheny's room and there were two dextrose bottles waiting to be changed. They were hanging up there nice and dark, and I thought of life and health, of calves getting their nourishment from milk replacer, of newborn lambs with their heads bobbing up to the milk.

I put the thermometer in Phil's mouth while he moved his left foot from one side to another. When I took it out he started to talk, but his foot kept right on moving.

"Hey Weaver, do you ever trim that beard?"

"*Ja.*"

"Why don't you shave it off?" He laughed. "Did anyone ever tell you that it looks like a patch of weeds?"

"It's a part of our religion. Grown men are supposed to grow beards because that's the way God created us, to have hair."

"Ya, well he kind of cheated you." Then he swore—in a happy way, the way Toots Hacker swore.

I didn't say anything more because I liked Phil and knew that he wanted to get better. But he was so unhappy. I fixed up a few more things in the room and then I asked him if I could get him anything more. I knew I probably wasn't able to get it for him, but I'd give him a chance to talk and that put him in a better mood. Even if he swore too much.

"No, I don't think you could help."

"*Vell,* if I can, let me know." I wished I could get him out of there because that's what he always wanted.

He swore angrily, "I'd like to get back to work. This lying on your back isn't for nothin'." Phil looked at his hip. "Especially if you've got a wife and kids at home. My hip could heal just as well at home. But, no, they want to have me here so they can experiment with me and steal from the insurance company," he said.

Phil moved from the doctors to the mayor, the city in general, the orderlies, the nurses, Sandy, and even to God. Just like breathing, he swore at all of them and how they were all against him. It was terrible but the only thing I could bring myself to say was to grunt like a pig. I probably should have told him to look on the positive side of things, but it didn't come to me like that. Anyway, I thought some of the things he said were right, but I didn't know what to do about them.

Finally he was quiet, and he seemed to feel down about having talked so bad and so long. He asked me, "Do you have children?"

"Naw, I'm not married."

He swore, "I wish they'd let my kids come up here. No wonder I'm not healing. They don't even let you see your kids. You get all nervous."

"*Ja,* I wish I could bring them up here for you."

"This is one helluva place; you'd think it was a jail." Phil's foot on his left leg was still moving back and forth like a nervous tiger in a cage.

"*Ja*, no children are allowed."

"What'd you do before you started this work?"

"Farmed."

Phil swore happily. "You're a farmer?"

"*Ja*."

"And you left the farm to work at this place?"

"*Ja*, had to."

"That's what I mean. This place is a jail. They get you in and you're caught. Those nurses," he whispered this part, "they don't even let you go to the john without asking permission. I know what you mean by farming; that's work. Like my work in construction for Borg Sterner. We build the big high rises. But what are you gonna do? They won't let me go back. I've been here for six weeks."

"*Ja vell*, it's a little different for me. I came because I'm a CO."

"What's that, Weaver?"

"Conscientious objector. Christians don't go to war so we work in the hospitals."

"Yellow, huh?" He took my arm and swore in my ear just as nice as he could. "Well, I still say they caught you. If those doctors would let me, I could walk on this leg, support my wife and kids. This place just gets you and won't let you go."

"*Ja*, I gotta go." I started for the door.

"Hey farmer, I like your beard."

"*Ja*."

"Let's get out of this place together." Phil laughed and swore some more at his hip and anything else that came in range. His right foot was still going back and forth like the tiger. That's the last thing I remembered when I thought of him, the way that foot was always moving.

I stroked my little scrubby hayfield beard as I went down the hall. Everyone seemed to notice it. Other men had short hair, flat tops, duck tails, or butches, but I had a beard and didn't shave it. My clothes looked like any *Englischer*, and I even bought one of those thin belts that were in style. My hair were shingled a little like the *Englischer*, but I wanted to grow a beard, even if it wasn't as nice and thick as it should have been and even if I hadn't joined the church yet.

I met Sandy in the hall again. She stopped and smiled at me, knowing full well that I was watching her. She looked in my eyes and I looked down a little. There were her breasts pointing right at me and accusing me of liking them.

"How is everyone?"

"Vell . . ." But she did not wait for me to finish. "Did you talk to Phil?" she asked.

"Ja."

"He's sick. His attitude is terrible."

"Ja, he wants to go home."

Her voice became softer. "It's a sad case. He's stupid and a sick man. He's crippled and he won't admit it."

"He'd like to see his children."

"A lot of good some little kids would do to his broken hip that won't heal."

"He wants to support his family."

"He needs rest, and he's too nervous."

"Ja." I thought of the tiger.

She smiled at me again and looked right in my eyes. Her black eyes bewitched me and they also trusted me. They reminded me of Anna's eyes, and I got sad, because I didn't want to even think of their eyes together. It was something how I thought of Anna at strange times, and sometimes I even cried. But the pain was not as hard now that I was away from home. And then I hoped I wasn't forgetting too easy. Sandy looked down at her watch.

"You need some coffee," she said. "Let's go over to the lounge."

I went to another room and got a tray and then followed Sandy to the lounge. I knew she thought she was leading me and that she enjoyed it, but I really didn't care. If I am here, she can lead. Why not? Here I am the visitor. If someone comes to Holmesburg and visits us, then I'll lead because I know the lay of the land. But here she knows the land, and anyway, she's a registered nurse and my boss.

She took a cup of coffee from the percolator and sat down, taking a deep breath. She pulled a pack of cigarettes out of her pocket and offered me one.

She smiled with her eyes twinkling. She knew better.

"Naw, thanks," I said.

"Come on, Weaver, you have to do something. You don't go to the movies; you don't smoke; you don't go to war; you don't bet. Look, you gotta do something."

Ja, I do, I thought. I look at your breasts. They point at me and I get excited. But I couldn't say that. Judas, she'd think I was a pervert or something. Anyway it was a depraved thought. I looked up into the corner of the ceiling. *"Ja,"* I said with a grin. "I do something."

She laughed, "Wayne, don't you think I'm a Christian too? And I don't even know how to — what do you call that going to bed together?"

I just kept a straight face. "Bundle," she giggled, remembering. "You still have to teach me to bundle."

"*Ja*."

"I also believe in God, Christ, the Holy Spirit and the Bible."

"Huh."

"And I don't know anything about buggies and bundling." She patted me as though I were some kind of pet rabbit. "And I can dance and smoke," she laughed.

"I see you can."

"Does that make me a sinner? Wicked?"

"I have to do what our church believes is right."

"Maybe your church is wrong. What if it doesn't understand the Bible? Your church is way behind the times. I mean, way back."

"The Bible says, 'Thou shalt not kill,'" I quoted. "It says to shun evil and flee from it. It says we should follow Christ and respect our elders. It's all in the Bible."

"But listen, how many of you are there? If you're right, why haven't others caught on?"

I put my head in my hands and tried to think. I had never counted how many were in our district. "I don't know exactly. Maybe 30 families in the Holmesburg East district." I added quickly, "And there are lots of other districts in Holmes County. There are Amish in Lancaster, Canada, Indiana and Iowa, too. Maybe there are over 50,000 Amish."

"Do you know how many people are in the rest of the world? Think of all the people in America — over 200 million — and then begin to think of China. And you're right and all the rest of us are wrong?"

"We have to do what we understand to be right."

She began to laugh when I said that. She wasn't being cruel; I just think it was funny to her. "Sometimes I pity you," she said.

"You don't need to. It's not that bad, if you're used to it." I wanted her to know we liked our way. "We enjoy our lives. And there are others like us." I thought for a minute. Should I tell her about Malcolm or the Mennonites?

"A Quaker visited us last summer and he believes the same way. He told me."

"How many Quakers are there?"

"Don't know, but he looked like everyone else, almost." I paused; no, I might as well not go into Malcolm anymore. "But the

Mennonites, they believe like us too."

"They wear beards and drive buggies too?"

"No, they're like you; they look kinda like you, but they act and believe like us. They're like you and they're like us. On the other hand, they're not like you and they're not like us. Just like that Quaker."

Sandy laughed some more. She blew puffs up in the air. "Wayne, you are something."

Ja, I am. I turned red and watched her breasts go up and down as she laughed. Judas, what had I just told her: flee every appearance of evil. This was an important conversation and then these two boobs get my attention. *Ach vell,* maybe I was talking too much anyway.

"*Vell,* we should all live up to the light that we have. If we do that, maybe sometime we'll get together," I said.

"Nice thought," she said laughing like a kitten. "I can always depend on you to say it sooner or later." She came right up to me and patted me on the cheek like I was Bounce or something. She smelled tremendous. I just turned red.

"Gotta go," I said and left. It was funny, I guess, because we didn't agree with each other, but we liked each other.

Sure, other people might not become like me, but should I become like them? Maybe Sandy and the nurses are right too. But that doesn't make sense either. If we're all right, then there's no wrong. You can only tell the right if you know the wrong. I won't try to figure it all out. I simply have to tell them: "*Vell,* people have to live up to the light that they have. If we all take that attitude, maybe we'll come together some day."

It wasn't my line. It was a line I had heard Chris say one day to a Canton newspaper reporter who was Jewish. The reporter didn't say anything, but you could see that he was satisfied. Chris told us that it was a good line for *Englischer* and outsiders who couldn't understand us. Chris was good with words.

I went to the nurses' station.

"They're ready in the emergency room," the head nurse told me.

I got the cart and went down the hall. In the ER several of the patients were ready to go, and I carted them to their rooms or to intensive care. On one of the emergency room operating tables lay an unconscious person with bandages across the chest and face. A young woman who moaned and groaned was lying on a second table. Be sure your sins will find you out, my dear students. *Vell,* that was the first thought that came to my mind, but I knew it was being too hard on them. The room was crackling with zip and importance the way the doctors and nurses were all business with work that was right next to the door of death.

The chief surgeon told us to wait a little because he was still working on the moaning woman, and he wanted to keep the man who was all wrapped up for a few minutes yet. I watched him cut and sew up the young woman's arm. From listening and asking questions I found out that there had been a music concert, and some of the students were up on a temporary scaffold and it had fallen. It was up where they had some of the loudspeakers, and they all came crashing down. The only thing I could imagine were the beams at a barn-raising and what would happen if they fell on the crowd. *Vell*, I knew I'd hear more of it later when I'd talk to these students.

Then the bandaged up young man was ready to go, and I carted him out of there. If ever anyone looked like Lazarus coming forth, he did. He was wrapped up, head and all. The only part that wasn't covered was his one eye. Still he was conscious, or so I thought, and the body seemed firm and strong. Too bad to have this happen to a young healthy man, but accidents are no respecters of persons. That was lesson number one of the hospital.

"He'll make it," a doctor told me as I wheeled him away.

I rolled the cart into the elevator, and that's when I thought there was something familiar about the body. Maybe this was something that came to me later, but I often asked myself why I didn't recognize him earlier. He had red hair and a strong and lean body. *Vell*, the rest was covered with the sheet and bandages so I couldn't see any more, but something told me to watch him.

In the elevator I thought of Anna. It was a sad thought, but I often had it when I wheeled people along like this. Someone had wheeled my friends around in the Claybourne Hospital in Dover only a few months ago. The lights blinked out for a minute when I pressed the button to the 10th floor. That's our life; it could be out in the flick of a light.

On the tenth floor Sandy and I put the young body on the bed. She took over then in checking him out and seeing that he was comfortable—I guess as comfortable as you can be when you're all banged up. Several times during the evening I made the rounds, looking after everybody. The evening sure went fast with all the commotion of the new people from the accident.

I had a good feeling, working those hours. It was right that I was working while the rest of the world was playing, resting or sleeping in the evening. Sandy and the nurses and the doctors and I would take care of the sick and the cripples, the winos, the cancer ridden and the careless drivers. If they fell from the scaffolds at concerts, we would take care of them.

At eleven o'clock, before I punched out, I went back to the room of the bandaged young man and checked on him one more time. He was still sleeping, and his parents were there looking at him and looking sad. The woman said to me: "Thank you for the good care you are giving to our son."

"*Ja, vell* I'm just trying to do my work."

"But it's loving care, and we appreciate it; Malcolm is our only son."

Then I knew it was him. I put my head down to the name tag on his arm and looked closely. Sure enough, it said "M. Smith." He stirred, and I slowly took his hand and squeezed it. And he squeezed mine back. I wasn't just imagining it; it was real and my whole insides were just like they had been flushed down the toilet. I had found my friend, and I was happy and drained, and I even forgot that he was hurt.

The nice woman got me out of my trance when she said to me: "Do you know him?"

"*Ja,*" I said very softly. "I know him." And then I walked out of the room and cried. I thought I'd explain it all to them later.

18.

Malcolm got better. He started to get strength in his legs and after getting black and blue as a thunderstorm, he began to turn normal colors. His skin was healing, and slowly we unwrapped him so that there were fewer bandages every day. They were going to do some plastic surgery. It was hard on him and hurt terribly.

I wasn't glad he got hurt, but it did give my work a new meaning, taking care of someone I knew. I worked the regular hours and sometimes stayed over longer or came in earlier to be in his room with him. I think it was partly because I wanted to help him out for the way that he had left us.

"You're the one person in Cleveland who is not always asking me questions."

"How's that?"

"Everyone wants to know about my beard or why we don't own cars. Is it true that we still bundle?" I laughed. "*Vell,* they only ask that if they know me a little bit like Sandy. Why don't we serve in the army? Aren't we enjoying this land of freedom and liberty? Then there's one woman who always wants to know if I'm saved. Do I plan to go back and join my people? Why don't we use tractors? And how do I know that we're right?"

"How do you like that? Being exhibit number one of the Holmesburg East District at Cleveland City?"

"Yup, I'm the top Holstein at the county fair. *Ja vell*, it isn't that bad," I said. "Most of these people have never met anything like me so they're interested. And they make me figure things out. I never had to think about how we did things back home. It was just the way it was. You farmed with horses because that's the way everyone else did it. Your father did it that way and all your neighbors did and so you did it that way. *Vell*, not the English, but the ones who mattered."

"Here your neighbors are different."

"I think I understand Gravey Ben a little better now too."

"The preacher with the bright blue eyes?"

"The same one. He's known to be the strict one in the district, especially since it hit him as bishop. He has kind of a name with the young people and everyone knows that Joseph is the gentle one."

"Joseph had the soft watery eyes, didn't he?"

"*Vell*, I believe so," I said. "I don't usually tell people apart that much by the eyes, but anyway on Gravey. He once went out to the West Coast when he was young and then he went to Florida for some winters. They say he was really *litterlich*.

"Really the wild one. People said that he had nothing to do with our people and was once even thrown in jail for fighting. Kind of like my brother Roy.

"But there's Gravey," I said getting back to Gravey. "Here he is a bishop and a strong one at that. *Vell*, see, I think he did some thinking while he was living and tearing around out in the world, and when he decided to join the church he knew what he was leaving and what he was joining."

I told Malcolm then that I liked to tell him these kind of things because he knew what I was talking about.

"How's that?" he asked.

"Did you ever try to explain something to people, but they don't understand your background and how you think and so you keep explaining but you never get any place?"

"For example?"

"You take courtship. Everyone likes to get on the subject of our courtship."

"Well, I don't know much about the social life," he said, looking down.

I dropped my eyes to the floor and felt like dreck, pure dirt. "I'm sorry about that. That wasn't right and all what happened at Sol Troyers. I should have stepped in and helped you. That was just *litterlich* the way those drunks acted. And there I stood like some

Judas."

Malcolm tried to make me feel better. "I should never have gone," he said.

"*Ja*, I should have told you and Leona to stay away."

He butted in: "But you did. We just didn't listen."

"Doesn't matter," I said. I guess I could have told him that Leona still thought they did the right thing in going, but I didn't want to go into that.

"I guess they didn't want an outsider around," said Malcolm.

"*Vell*, there's something there. Just a few weeks before an *Englischer* had hit one of the Buwe's buggies with his car and then beat up the Amish guy, claiming he had no right to be on the road with that slow rattle trap. So the *Buwe* were a little mad, and edgy as wounded bulls. But they were drunk and threw nonresistance out the window, and it's no good. Naw, no good."

"Could you prop my foot up a little more? It fell off the pillow." I went to the foot of the bed and put it back in place. It was still plenty swollen and black and blue. I looked at my hands and how they had changed. Just a few months ago those hands were calloused, strong and rugged. Now they were white, soft, clean and, *vell*, I hoped still gentle. It was something the difference between handling pitchforks, plow handles and working with hay and thistles and this handling sheets, feet, beds and glasses.

I loosened his bandage at the knee a little and did a few more things before going. "You sure got punished for listening to music."

"I've heard the Kingston Trio many times in my dreams. You might like them." Then he told me all about folk music and how his parents would bring me one of the records if I wanted to hear them. I told him it sounds a little like hillbilly to me, but he claimed it was different, and he went into a lot more background than I could ever explain.

"Anyway, you really fell for it," I said.

"One day we are here and the next we are gone, or we are hurt, or we move to another place. It simply happens to us. As though we were like your brother Benny. He doesn't plan, and things just happen. I plan, but few things turn out like I expected or wanted them to. Do you ever feel you are as helpless as your little brother Benny?"

"I hadn't thought of it that way," I said. At least I wasn't in a mood to talk about it now.

"I mean, what did I do to deserve being put on my back for

several months and to have all this plastic surgery? What did you do to deserve having your best friend killed? You didn't do anything that bad. Give me one good reason why Anna should have died."

Judas, this was enough. I had gone through this earlier. Pretty soon he was going to see only clouds and become a candidate for Massilon.

"*Ja vell*," I said, "now listen. And what did I do to deserve having Dad and *die Memm* who send me food and welcome me home whenever I go there? What did I do to have a church that supports me and is good to me? What did I do to get to work here in this hospital instead of having to go to an army camp? I heard stories of those who lived through the First World War."

I knew that I was getting way too excited so I tried to calm down a little. I said in a soft voice, "By cracky, I tell you that I'm thankful to God for these things that he does for us."

"That certainly is the good side of it," he said.

"No-sir-ee. This is the important side of it," I told him. "That God gives us life and that we can have so many blessings from him. You have good parents, too, and friends; I see them come to visit you. Your own life here is a miracle. The way you were banged up. By gum, I thought surely you would die."

"Yes, at least I'm alive."

"You're tootin' right, and instead of whining like some spanked dog, you should be thankful." I knew this was too strong, but it just came out like that.

We were both quiet then for several minutes. I lifted his foot again and put it comfortably on the pillow. I looked at the clock and saw that it was already past midnight and we both should get some sleep. Anyway, when you get on this what is the meaning of life you can go for a day and still not get any further.

"Would you do one thing before you go?" he said, and then he made the easiest request I ever answered. He asked me to read one of the Psalms. I took one of the Gideon Bibles from the drawer and started to read Psalm 22:

My God, my God, why hast thou forsaken me?
why art thou so far from helping me,
and from the words of my roaring?
O my God, I cry in the daytime,
but thou hearest not;
and in the night season,
and am not silent.

It had 31 verses and when I got to Psalm 23, the Shepherd Psalm, his eyes were closed and he was breathing softly, but I kept on reading. At the end of the 24th Psalm I stopped. We had passed through the valley of the shadow of death and the Shepherd's rod and the staff had comforted us. I was getting sleepy myself.

I looked at Malcolm's relaxed face and his deep breathing; his red hair was hanging from the side of his face and his beard was stubbly. When I looked up from the bed, there at the door stood Sandy. I don't know how long she had stood there or how much she had heard of me reading.

Sandy just looked at me a while and then she looked at the sleeping man, and then she came over to me. "I was going to get another blood sample," she said softly. "But we'll let him sleep now." Then she left just as quietly as she had come in. I put the Bible away, and I think it was the first time that I really knew that the Heavenly Shepherd had some red and some black lambs too.

After that I sometimes read to him in the evenings from the Psalms and the Gospels, and I even recited to him some of the poems I had memorized in school, like "The Village Blacksmith" and "The Song of Hiawatha." I couldn't remember quite all of them right away, but they came to me. I think I was a little like David when he helped Saul from going completely crazy. I even read a little to Phil Cheny and he said he liked to hear my voice.

Malcolm's fever stayed on for a while longer and the pain from the skin grafting was terrible. But he was also healing and I didn't think he had as many of those dark thoughts.

On election night, Malcolm's parents brought a portable TV to his room and I stayed up with him to see the election returns. Kennedy won and Malcolm was glad. "He's more humane and smarter than Nixon," he said.

"No good," I said. "He's a Catholic."

"What's wrong with being Catholic? That's like saying you're no good because you're Amish."

"*Ja vell*, we all have to do what we understand to be right. I hope Kennedy does that too."

19.

We went fox hunting on New Year's weekend. It was my first time back home since September when I left. Maybe I'll never go back to stay, I thought, if I keep on changing as much as I have these first few months. It was a good thought that made me feel free and like I could do a lot of things, but it also made me wonder about if this was the way that Roy changed and if this was the way that people lost their convictions.

I had worked on Christmas Day and had even volunteered to fill in on an extra shift so that others could take more time off with the family. *Vell,* somebody had to run the shop, the way Sandy would say, and anyway if some of the soldiers had to be out at their barracks on Christmas, why couldn't I be doing something good?

I got a fox in the morning on our first hot scent and then spent the rest of New Year's Day chasing cold trails on the Hershberger's back-40. The family was at the chores that evening when I came home. Everybody but *die Memm* was in the barn helping with the evening milking.

When I opened the sliding door, John was squirting milk to the tom who drank it right out of the air. When he saw me he began to milk like the dickens. I acted as if I didn't notice; my brother was still growing up. Benny came running to me and grabbed me around the waist.

"Get one, huh?" said John.

"*Ja*, he ran right near me down in the gully in the McCollough fields." Already before I got home everyone knew about my fox.

I walked on and came to Leona and Ben who were milking away toward the middle of the line of stanchions. "There are still a few down at the end," said Leona.

"*Vell*, is there a pail?"

"*Ja*, out in the milk house."

I pointed at Leona's pail and sent Benny off to get it. "This will give your white hands a good workout before you go back to the soft work," said Leona. "It's a good way to begin the New Year."

"An orderly does some lifting too," I said.

"Like glasses of water."

"Bodies."

"Thermometers."

"Now listen," I said it in a serious tone. "It's more than you think. You lift people, some heavy ones too, from one bed to another. But the glasses of water are important too. You don't realize how helpless people can get till you're flat on your back. Then you appreciate it, even when you do the little things for them, like pulling up the sheet or, *ja*, giving a glass of cold water."

Leona looked up at me, and I could see that she wanted to tell me something. Ben was at the next cow and didn't say a word but just kept on milking like all Sam Hill.

"*Ja vell*, you really like your work up there. I can tell and I'm glad. Maybe sometime I can leave for a while too and work at a nursing home or maybe even at the Millersville or Wooster Hospital. You know, when we have more help here."

"*Ja*, you would like that. You'd be good at that work." Benny came and stood right beside me, and we both just stood there with the pail.

"You're 18 now."

"Almost."

"Maybe there'll be some other reasons for leaving," I said. I knew that she had been dating a Raber fellow from up in Stark County and that both Dad and *die Memm* liked him.

"Naw, we don't know where it'll go."

But she looked at me in a way that I knew she had thoughts in the wild blue yonder. Maybe she wanted to settle down with this decent Raber fellow or maybe she was hoping for work at a hospital, but it was the first I realized that Leona would go too and that the house was getting empty.

She was silent for a little and then she looked up at me again. "Do you ever think of Anna?" And she kept right on going. "I do. I still dream of that night, that bad night we went to Wheeling."

"*Ja*, it was a bad dream."

"I should have known better than to go like that."

"*Vell*, we can always look back, but some things we'd probably just as well not try to explain. It wasn't your fault." I felt sorry for her because there was nothing to do about it.

"You probably never can forgive Roy for what happened that night."

"Naw."

"You mean you don't hold it against him?" she asked.

"Naw," I said, but I felt helpless and lonely as Benny held me closer. I put the pail down and squeezed my retarded brother close to me. He stank like a muskrat, but it didn't make a thing out. "He's as sorry as I am, and it just makes me sad when I think that he could have gone another way. Remember how he used to bring us ice cream when he came home from work with the construction gang?"

"Did you know who showed up this afternoon? His wife and child."

"Don't say."

"*Ja*, this Akron woman drives in and she's got a little *Bubbli* that sure had the pointed Weaver nose."

"*Vell*, I'd heard he has some wife and child."

"*Ja*, she said Roy sends her money and is good to her, but with Christmas and some extra doctoring they were in bad shape."

"Did you help her?" I said to my father.

"What else could I do?" Ben was milking furiously. "You can't turn away the children."

"*Bubbli*," said Benny. "*Bubbli*."

Leona told me later that they had given her plenty, including some canned food and fruit. I went to the cow at the end of the line. I cleaned her udder with warm water. Then slowly I took two squirts onto the cement floor. A cat came to lick up the milk. I put the clean aluminum pail between my legs and slowly began the rhythms of pulling and squeezing the teats. Foam showed up on the top of the milk as it rose in the pail. Gradually my hands picked up speed, and then they slowed down again. I felt warmed by my moving and by my closeness to the cow. My hands got tired, and I knew I wasn't in practice. It seemed so easy, like I had done this since my baby years, yet at the same time it had become strange in only a few months.

I started on the back teats. Again I began slowly and gradually picked up speed, from deep pulls and squeezes to short fast squirts. I went up and down, and Janet couldn't have let the milk down any nicer until the three-gallon pail was almost full and her udder was empty. I took some long deep squeezes to finish her off, and oh was I tired. I looked up and there was my father.

Ben was standing behind the cow and right in front of me. He looked worn and weary. All at once it hit me that Dad had worked long and hard for 60 years and was getting beat like my hands. He was our gruff and forceful family leader, but that night I saw that he was old and his eyes looked tired.

"You still do it well," he said.

"*Ja.*"

"I need you."

"Huh?"

"*Ja,* I need you when you finish up there in Cleveland." Benny came over to our father then and stood beside him, standing straight as a board and trying to be good. My old man put his arm around my little brother's shoulders, and I could have cried.

"I'm getting on in years, and this place is too big. There's too much work here. When you finish 1-W John will soon have to go, and then I'm alone. The older ones have their farms. I lost Roy, and it'll be only *die Memm* and Benny and me. Leona, you just heard Leona. She wants to go too."

"*Ja.*"

"We need you here."

"Huh."

After that I milked two more cows, but I wasn't thinking of milking anymore. It was as if in that short talk with my father, my future became clear and I was happy as a lark in the spring. My father needed me. I wasn't just in Cleveland to see what would happen. I was there to do the best I could with the sick, and then I'd come back and give my parents a hand. They needed me.

After that evening even Anna's death seemed different. I used to live for a home and a marriage and that farm I'd dream about on the way home on Sunday mornings. Then I lived with the sadness of having all that go away, and deep down I hoped it could happen again. It took my father, who always took care of himself and of us, to teach me that the most important thing is to give to others. That's what I was learning at the hospital and that's what came to me now: "I need you."

By the time we left the barn it was pitch dark. A bright moon outlined the big clapboard farmhouse among the trees. I saw the kerosene light through the kitchen window, and my mother's shadow flicking past it.

I went upstairs and got my clothes together and packed. *Die Memm* loaded me up with some *schnitz* pie and cheese and balogna, and John and I went out and hitched Flecha to the buggy. I saw Ben watching from the porch. Leona waved a quick flicker of the fingers, the very way *die Memm* often does.

John took me in to Chris and Martha's where I spent the night to catch the 5:10 bus in the morning. Flecha ran sure and fresh on the cold hard road, snorting while puffing in the frosty night air, always looking for more rein.

"You take good care of her, John," I said.

"You betchyourboots," said John and I knew he'd do just that.

At four o'clock I heard sounds of breakfast in the kitchen below. Martha had some coffee and cocoa and corn mush with applesauce for us. "You won't get this in Cleveland," she said to me as I came to the table. She put some homemade grapenuts in a bag and sent it along too.

Although we could have walked, Chris and the boys harnessed Bess and took me to Holmesburg to get the bus. The ducks squawked and the drakes hissed as the buggy woke them up when we buttered out the drive.

The moon was still high up in the grey morning sky. A stray dog came wandering down the street and stopped to look at us and then he went on.

"Too bad you have to go back," Chris said to me.

"Naw, I want to go."

"Don't say."

"I like it there. My work is there, and they need me."

"But it's such a place," said Chris.

"*Ja vell.*"

"But you'll come back."

"Sure," I said.

"*Ja vell,* of course."

"Only can do one thing at a time." Just then the gruff but spent face of my father came to my mind. "Dad needs me. I am a farmer."

"*Ja vell.*"

The large diesel engine of the Greyhound was roaring toward

the red light on the square. The driver shifted down, and I went to pick up my bags. Chris shook my hand when I turned around.

"Make it good," he said.

"Will do," I said, and winked to my little nephews as I got on the bus.

Chris and the boys went for the buggy.

About the Author

Levi Miller was born into an Amish family in 1944 in Holmes County, Ohio, the largest community of Old Order Amish in the world.

He studied American literature at Malone College (B.A.) and Bowling Green State University (M.A.). Currently he is program director at Laurelville Mennonite Church Center in western Pennsylvania.